DISASTERS

IN THE

FIRST WORLD

DISASTERS

IN THE

FIRST WORLD

STORIES

OLIVIA CLARE

Black Cat
New York

For Lula Clark

CONTENTS

DISASTERS

IN THE

FIRST WORLD

PÉTUR

Ash fell from the wind. She began to take long walks. Before breakfast, after lunch, she walked the weed-pocked path to the lake. White ash turned the lake's surface to desert and the tops of fjalls invisible.

By the third morning, ash from Eyjafjallajökull coated the porch, the porch rail, the seats of the porch chairs, and the rented station wagon. The *hrossagaukur* had flown off, and the cabin's weather vane creak had stopped. Laura told Adam, again, she was going out. He was her son. She tied a gauze scarf around her nose and mouth.

"I look like a robber," she said.

"No one will see you."

He opened the door for her into the otherworldly weather. She was garish in the ash in her green flannel coat. At the cabin window, he watched her diminish, and like a little boric flame a quarter mile away, her back rose on the path, then shrank and went out.

This dale in Iceland had a permanent population of eighty-six. They had seen almost no one—once or twice, before late sunset at nine o'clock, they'd heard shouting children. Icebabies, Laura called them. You can't ever see them, of course. They're made only of sound.

Adam was a data systems analyst. He was thirty-six. He lived in a one-bedroom apartment in Palo Alto. It was tiny and out of the way, on the other side of town from Laura's house, which she'd once shared with his father. Iceland for two weeks had been her idea for her birthday. She'd just turned sixty-one, and she told Adam she didn't believe it, and he shouldn't't, either. She'd said, You look in the mirror and acknowledge you're as old as you like. She felt nineteen, mostly. She looked fifty.

She returned from her walk late enough that Adam had made soup. The cabin had five rooms, floors of dull old wood, a kitchen and dining area adjoining the living room. There was a woodstove, a coffee table with a fan of women's fashion magazines, an expensive guitar on its stand, a box of black rocks and cockles from the lake, a striped sofa, a ripped cushion. They were renting the cabin from a family who'd advertised the place online.

"On the news they're saying don't go out at all," he said.

"But no one's said anything like that to me." She lowered her scarf from her face to her neck.

Bits of ash stuck to the silvering blonde roots of her hair. She was tall, too slim. She wore blue jeans and boots.

"On TV, Mother." He put a roll and a bowl in front of her, soup with halibut and celery from the store in town. She was still shaking from the cold.

"Well, people are out there," she said. "I talked to some people."

"Who's out there? Rangers?"

"I think it's coming down most at the lake," she said. "Right now it's like the moon. It's not dangerous on the moon." She untied the scarf and put it on the dining room table. "Come with me, come to the lake."

"It's unhealthy."

She picked up a chunk of fish in her spoon. "What does antimatter mean?"

"What?"

"What's antimatter?"

"Antimatter?" Adam wiped his mouth with his napkin. "Sure, it's like a mirror image, a negative image of matter, like matter's twin. And there are antiprotons. Antielectrons—"

"What happened to all the fish?" she said.

"In the lake? All dead, from the ash."

"I don't think they feel anything."

She walked in, waking Adam from a nap in a chair beside the fire in the woodstove. Her scarf was tangled around her neck. Her green coat off, a rip in her shirt at the elbow. She held her arm to her chest: a bright red cut like a seam showed through the rip. She went into the bathroom with a sleepwalker's involuntary smile and an alien tannic scent, maybe wine.

"You're going to laugh," she shouted, "when I tell you what happened."

"Let me help you," he said, getting up from the chair.

"It's fine," she said. "Sit down. It doesn't hurt."

Maybe she'd stolen a neighbor's skiff, as she had the week before, the day they had argued because he looked out the window and said a fjall was beautiful. She'd told him not to call things that, told him that one word, *beautiful*, a word his father had used constantly, was limiting. She had learned the landscape, the words *rill, caldera,* and the names of wildflowers. Nights after her afternoon walks, she would sit with a field guide. I have a bird heart, she'd say, your mother, the bird. Precise knowledge of a fjall's origins, or of the call each bird made, was the closest she felt to wisdom, because *land,* because details, she said, were important. They were solid and finite and felt infinite.

"Let me help you," Adam said again. "Please."

She came back into the room. "I was climbing up that boulder on the shore. I had my camera with me and a bird swooped near my head, and I tumbled off. Your mother. On the ground."

"No more walks."

"I wasn't going to," she said.

"It's like with those eggs in California. You had that accident when you reached for the nest. You forget what you're doing."

She looked at him, expecting a response. What did she want? He knew how she thought of him, his normalcy. She said what she thought, and there was both innocence and maturity in that. When she was eleven, she'd told him, she had watched her brother die from a rare leukemia. She spent the rest of her life trying to strike lightning back.

"Don't worry," she said. "The eggs were fine. They were alive."

"I believe you," he said.

Laura had raised him on her "wisdom and whims"—she had taken him to museums and operas, he'd had a violin and no television, she'd taught him the names of native ferns and trees around their house. Sometimes she had invented names. On Adam's first day of high school, she'd taken his face in her hand and told him school was for wolves and sheep, that

4

wolves and sheep ought to be separate, and that she wanted him to be a wolf. She was a wolf. His father was a sheep.

He'd attended college in Connecticut, joined a fraternity, been an average student. He visited her that first Christmas, then stopped. He stayed on after school and got a job in Bridgeport. When they talked on the phone, she told him he'd become something else, someone she didn't understand.

Four years after he graduated, Laura called him: they'd found a small tumor in her neck. He flew to Palo Alto to live with her awhile. She'd said it wasn't necessary. He had rented a small apartment and got a job there, told himself he'd been planning to live in California eventually and that it was the right thing to do. She recovered fully, incredibly. Now he saw her for every Sunday dinner, some weeks more frequently to help around the house, though she claimed she didn't need him.

He aged uneventfully. Gained a little weight, lost a little hair. He was often ill with some nonthreatening flu or infection; he had problems with his joints. He saw several doctors and specialists. Sometimes he had a girlfriend, and there was a coworker he slept with occasionally.

But Laura—she'd become younger, uncommonly healthy. Woke earlier, stayed up later, ate what she wanted, was always hungry. It was as if she was subtracting years. Some days she told him her ecstatic dreams, which never contained people.

After dinner she stood on the sofa and took down the three framed watercolors on the living room walls.

"Be careful," he said.

"It's just that they're a bit disgusting. Kitsch." She balanced on the back of the sofa, her feet clinging to the edge. She'd painted her toenails pink the night before. "I should have done this the day we got here."

"They're not ours."

"I refuse to stare at them anymore. It's unhealthy." She jumped off the sofa without trouble and stacked the watercolors in a corner and looked around the room for anything else that offended her. She took the fashion magazines from the coffee table and put them in a drawer.

"I think I'll go for a walk," she said.

"Please don't."

"Please don't tell me don't."

"Mother. Don't go outside."`

"You love scolding me. You think you get something from it. Like your father."

"All right," he said. "Then I'll come with you."

They walked to the lake with scarves tied around their faces—he'd insisted, though the ash had stopped falling. Anyway, it was cold, he said. It was mid-April. He could hardly see the other cabins, spaced around the dale, in the northern pre-twilight. Another constellation of cabins, mirroring their own, was across the lake. A giant fjall above them.

She had been asking to come to Iceland for years, ever since she'd met an Icelandic man, divorced and in his fifties. After she'd recovered from her illness, she had started seeing him, and then had stopped abruptly. But she still needed to visit the place that felt like both "the end of this world and the beginning of another," as the man had told her. Adam wouldn't let her travel by herself. What a good son you are, they'd said to him at work. Your mother's very lucky. He'd felt he had no choice.

6

He was quiet while they walked, he knew that was important to her, but he wanted to say something about the red blinking light across the lake—the rangers' station—and the sound of the skiffs knocking against one another, tied on the shore. He felt practical. He felt he wasn't there.

"God," he said finally.

"What?"

"Everything. We're trapped. A volcano erupted, we're trapped."

"We have a car," she said.

"It needs gas. It's a hundred dollars here for a tank, you know. A hundred twenty-five."

"I see."

She didn't. The trip had cost him thousands. She owned her house in California outright, had a small pension from Adam's father, and Adam took care of the rest. She knew nothing of money; she'd forget to pay bills. She'd bought a car she couldn't afford. Here, of course, but even in California, she acted as though currency were foreign to her. At restaurants, she treated money as if it were only paper, holding it by the corners. She left waiters incredible tips.

"We're not trapped," she said.

"We are," he said. "That's the perfect word for what we are."

"Think of this as something else, meaningful. Maybe this is a land of ash now. This is some kind of other place. Ashland."

She was asking him to concede, to play her game, as she'd asked him to imagine things when he was a child. He wouldn't anymore. He said nothing, and she looked at him with disappointment, as if he had played the wrong notes on the piano. But in fact he'd played nothing.

They'd come to the lake, a layer of ash on the surface, gray-white. Torn bits of paper. She took off one of her shoes and put a toe in the shallow water. Specks of ash stuck to her pink toenails. She let her whole foot sink in.

"Isn't it too cold?" he said.

"We're not trapped," she said.

"We're trapped in a volcano. It's remarkable."

"It isn't remarkable. Nothing is merely remarkable. You think something can be one word," she said, taking off her other shoe and standing with both feet in the lake. "You can enjoy yourself. Not think the way you do. You're not always just who you think you are."

She spoke softly, as if to herself. Her inflections were neutral, anonymous, any evidence of her midwestern origins gone. She had sung with a band in the seventies in Ohio, she often told him. Music producers had been interested, but her own mother had been jealous of any success, of any attention she'd received.

"Look, I'm tired," he said.

"Everyone I know is always tired."

"I'm sorry," he said.

She looked at him—a stranger's doubt and maternal empathy—and he wanted to ask her to either hug him, as sentimental as it was, or leave him alone. An act of kindness, or nothing at all.

"Your father said it that way. You never heard him say it."

"We should walk back now," he said.

In the morning Adam drove to the base of the dale with his laptop on his thighs, bumping against the steering wheel. The wagon's tires crushed sprigs of lupine powdered with days-old ash. Parked across from the ranger station, he leeched its

Internet and e-mailed clients. They were scheduled to return to Palo Alto in two days, but he knew they couldn't leave by then. The road to Reykjavík was closed indefinitely.

He had been gone a half hour and was driving back, when, rounding a switchback, he saw Laura two hundred feet below, a little green coat in high boots. She used a bowed branch as a walking stick. She carried a backpack he'd never seen.

He parked the car on the side of the road, tied his scarf around his face, and followed her down the path to the lake, through the tangle of bushes. She hadn't seen him, he was sure of it, but she walked as if pursued.

At the lake he hid behind a boulder. She crouched amid drifts of ash on the black rock shore. Hands quick as a sharp's dealing cards, she seemed to sort rocks into two stacks, then scooped a stack into her backpack and kicked the other into the lake. She was talking to herself—he'd caught her doing this before, at the cabin, washing her hands at the sink, gesturing to herself with the water running, talking and singing to no one, without words, cooing. Sometimes he thought she was too forgetful and scattered, too unpredictable. He worried he couldn't help her.

She left the lake. He followed her down another path, overgrown with wildflowers and weeds. She was walking up a stairway to a cabin. Weather-battered, smaller than theirs, with blue shutters. No antenna on the roof, no car in the gravel driveway lined with bushes. She knocked once, then opened the door herself, leaving stick and backpack on the porch.

Adam was heating soup when she returned, holding her scarf. She had the same preoccupied, sleepwalker's smirk, her blue jeans stained black at the cuffs. An inanimate vacancy in her eyes, wide-set as an elf owl's.

9

"What happened?" he said.

"I looked for fish, for anything living. There weren't any eggs out there, either."

She had been gone a few hours since he'd seen her enter the other cabin. Her backpack was gone. She put her scarf on the table and warmed her hands in the steam from his teacup.

"You were at the lake?"

"I can't see to its bottom. Looking at it that long makes me never want to look at land."

"Where's your backpack?" he said.

"I'll be back in a minute."

She went to her bedroom. He almost followed her; he went to the bathroom. Her cosmetics, her face powder, her tiny bronze cylinders of perfume were on the glass countertop. A canister of rouge had spilled. He collected the grains of rouge in a mound between his fingers and then released the mound into the sink. When she was ill, he'd had to help her to the bathroom. She'd put both arms around his neck while they walked. There is no gulf between humans wider than that between the ill and the well. When she was finished, she'd call for him to help her to the bed. She'd told him she had been trying to discover something unearthly, being nearer death. She couldn't find it. She'd told him he could have her pearls, her dog. Everything. How incredible, impossible, that she was completely well now and did not need him.

The light was off in her bedroom, but before he reached the doorway he heard her talking to herself, so softly he couldn't make out the words. It seemed as if she was trying to calm herself. He could smell her, the lotion she used on her face: lavender, clean. She sat on the bed.

"Mother?"

10

"Is there soup left?" she said, when she saw him. She looked startled. "For tomorrow's lunch?"

"What were you doing?" he said. He switched on a lamp in the room. He moved to touch her, and her shoulder tensed. He moved away.

"What?" she said.

"I saw you," he said. "In that house. You told me you'd stop going outside."

"I don't think I said that."

"I saw you go in that cabin."

"Pétur lives there, by himself. I met him one time, walking."

"But you agreed with me," he said. "It isn't healthy."

He wanted her to say it now, to say she agreed, to apologize.

"Pétur," she said, "has turned into a friend, I think."

She looked past him, toward the door. She was done talking. He saw in her face she intended to dismiss him. With her, you could risk nothing. She forgave nothing, not the slightest imposition upon the complex world she believed in. She saw that he was simple, he thought, ordinary. It scared him to watch her that way. Scared him more to watch her watch him that way.

Adam slept the kind of skeletal, half-sleeping wakefulness that allowed him the belief he was asleep. A car door somewhere in the dale closed, and he glanced at the digital clock, then turned on the TV. All European flights were stranded, and cots and cotless irate passengers crowded Heathrow terminals. Eyjafjallajökull had erupted a second time, ash descended on London and Scotland, and there was concern about Katla, another volcano, in Vík í Mýrdal.

"Could you turn it off?" Laura called from her room.

She left the cabin before he rose. The tattoo of her boots on the wood floor.

11

* * *

He came into a sheer fog at the end of the path. It was very early. There were no lights on in the cabins, most of them probably empty.

The lake was now dusted with faint patches of ash. He hadn't been able to convince himself not to follow her. He stopped at a boulder too tall to sit on and tightened the scarf around his face. The water, hitting the edge of the boulder, sprayed up in a small spire. The lake was the color of weathered nickel. Rocks like globules of oil littered a shallow bed at the shore. Across the lake, the other cabins were dark, too. A waterfall, tiny from where he stood, forked a few feet from the top of the fjall.

He walked the same path he'd seen her walk the day before. Bugs nagged his arms. He passed abandoned cabins; some had yards with patio furniture. In one yard was a yellow plastic toy car with ash on its roof.

He came to the bottom of the steps he'd seen her climb. Pétur's steps. Trees obscured the house. From the bottom of the stairs, Adam could see only the housetop, the woodstove chimney.

There was a table on the porch. A small gas grill. He stepped over an open garbage bag spilled on its side. He decided, without really considering, to crouch below a screened window and to look in with one eye.

Adam could see his mother at the other end of the house. She was alone, putting pots on the stove, her lips in motion. The cabin was one room, much smaller than theirs, with hardly any furniture. A table with chairs, a bed, an armchair in the corner, no refrigerator, dark rhombuses on the wall where

12

DISASTERS IN THE FIRST WORLD

frames had been. He could hear her now, talking quickly. He studied the interior. She was alone.

On the floor were her green flannel coat and the backpack he'd seen the other day. Rocks she'd collected from the shore were stacked in a pyramid and placed as a centerpiece on the table. Open cans on the counter, cans he recognized from their house, cans he'd bought at a nearby town store. She was talking, and he made out not the words, but the tone, the cooing inflection.

She became very quiet. He watched from the window. She brought a bowl of dim liquid to the table and ate, closing her eyes. He watched this a long time. She put her bowl and spoon in the sink. Then she pulled her dress over her head. She had on a pale slip. She took off her rings. On the bed, she climbed on top of nothing, of no one himself, and moved her hips forward and back.

The Visigoths

I let myself in with the key. Dark cumulus carpet stains, half-eaten fast food and burn marks on the coffee table, video games and consoles, plastic eyedrop containers, cereal boxes, instant pasta. Above the TV, a poster of a long line of ectomorphic college cheerleaders. Blake's bedroom door, decorated with scuff marks and boot-made dents, was closed.

"Come out," I said.

He made his teachers "nervous"; he corrected them. He remembered and recited beginnings of 1950s dime store novels, batting averages of dozens of baseball teams, Latin names of spider species in Chile and Tanzania, and he knew paintings, about which he did and didn't care. He was thirteen. Our mother, Deedee, had him entertain dinner guests—yes, sir, the etymology of *error* is *wander*. Delilah didn't shave off Samson's hair, her servant did. Domodossola, in Piedmont, was conquered in 12 BCE by the Romans; the Romans themselves were sacked by the Gauls, the Normans, the Visigoths, the Vandals.

"What?" I could hear him on the other side of the door, his voice still slightly high. "No."

"Come out right now."

"I can't."

"I drove out here just to see you."

"I drove out here just to see you." When he didn't know what to say, he mimicked you.

"I'm serious," I said.

"That's right."

"Blake. It's okay."

"Thank you, and have a nice day."

"Let me see you."

"I smell," he said.

Deedee had called me from work, worried about Blake. He's my half brother, fifteen years younger, born to Deedee and her second ex-husband. Blake lived with Deedee and her third husband, an oral surgeon, a consummate Dullard (what Blake and I called him). Blake opened the door in his long stained undershirt and glasses with lenses so thin they seemed not there.

He liked pornography, the Internet. He liked explosions, chase scenes, TV shoot-'em-ups and crashes, gang fights on the local news. Social networking sites, pop songs and rap, sitcom reruns in the afternoons. He hoarded gumballs, fruit sours, Sixlets, jelly beans, lollipops, Lemonheads. Weeknights he watched adult cartoons.

Deedee let him stay in the guesthouse, behind the main house. She thought this made her a good mother, progressive. There was a sheetless king-sized mattress on his bedroom floor, something chaotic and colorful on the bedroom TV. He stood, waiting for some end to come to this moment that, like most moments, was merely stalling him—he waited to return to whatever it was people like me kept him from, and I told him to shower, right now, and he did.

16

It was summer; I was twenty-eight and recovering from the previous year. I called myself a painter but didn't paint. Deedee gave me some money. I taught adult art classes at the community center and was compensated so little that I couldn't have my car's air-conditioning repaired. I apologized to Blake on the drive—he just looked out the window.

His counselor's office specialized in teenagers, anxiety, attention deficit, autism, social anxiety, eating disorders, obsessive-compulsive, the menu. In the waiting room was a generic, framed Escher spiral staircase, eighties rock on a boom box, overlaid by sound from a saucer-shaped white-noise maker in a corner. Well-browsed women's magazines on the table.

"This really is obscene," said Blake, gesturing to the waiting room as if showing me a museum piece. His arm was so thin and breakable—we were both smaller than average, something we'd inherited from Deedee.

"Did you know that ninety-eight percent of women are dental hygienists? Interesting? Relevant? Or who the hell cares? Your thoughts on this, please, Miranda." He took a pamphlet from the little rack, tightly rolled it up, and held it to my mouth.

"Well, what you have to remember is that what we think of as hell is just a Judeo-Christian construction," I said into the microphone. He seemed satisfied.

A boy sat beside us, eyes closed, dreamily stroking the in-flamed rims of his nostrils. On the other side of the room, a girl was hunched over, her hands between her knees, and two other kids, with their parents, watched their phones, scrolling and tapping, in front of a sign that read CELL PHONE USE IS NOT PERMITTED IN MENTAL HEALTH and another that read IF YOU SEE SOMETHING, SAY SOMETHING.

17

"That's true about cell phones," said Blake, taking off his glasses to clean them with his shirt.

The counselors, women and men in shabby business casual clothing, all Gen X and Baby Boomers, retrieved their patients one by one, looking apologetic, their mouths turned down, a universal expression: *I'll do what I can.* These were the people who'd eroded their patients, who'd realized the mistake too late, who tried to build them up again, but without clarity— witch doctors wandering far from the ruins of Freud. Each child left the room and each time, in me, there was a little ache.

Now Blake and I were alone in the waiting room. "Let's steal something," he said.

I would play most games he asked me to. I took a large stack of diabetes pamphlets and put them in my purse, then took a particularly thick pamphlet on domestic violence—a man's hands clamped around a woman's bruised face—and sat on it. There were pamphlets on medication. Blake went up to the unattended check-in desk and slowly, slowly tore the last week of August from a calendar.

"And don't forget to bring condoms," he said, kneeling like a knight in front of my chair and offering me the torn week.

"Inappropriate," I said.

"Sorry." He smiled. "And have a nice day."

Zoloft and Paxil and Prozac. Cymbalta and Klonopin. SSRI. This is the language of friends of mine from college. Daily pills to save them from defeat. Kate's grandfather died. Leigh had a miscarriage, a sister in a car crash. Johannes simply had bad dreams. I once told him I disliked my own bad dreams but didn't wish them gone. I could watch myself living all the parts of my life—ecstatic, painful—and I wanted all parts, all threads, even the unraveled.

Blake's counselor arrived, younger than the others, her facial features so delicate she seemed a child herself. When they left for her office, I pumped sanitizer onto my hands from a bottle on the table and rubbed. He sent me a text message from inside: "Such a rebel! Using my cell phone in the mental health!"

"Me too!" I replied.

After a while, the counselor came to take me to him.

"I'm Kerry," she said, closing the office door and sitting at her desk. "You can sit right there." Her voice made me think she was my age or younger.

Blake sat next to her and faced me, too, across the desk. I wondered if he enjoyed the attention from his doctors. He'd once told me: "You really have to give them a show, that's what they're here for."

Another saucer-shaped white-noise maker in the corner. Neutral carpet, fluorescent lighting, framed pastel floral prints. One of Kerry's eyes was red, with what could have been the beginning of a welt underneath. Maybe a husband or boyfriend had hurt her, had put his hands around her head. She seemed fragile, wistful. Maybe I could help her.

"He needs to set an alarm and take his medication in the morning," Kerry said. "If he takes it at night, he won't sleep."

"He could try a different serotonin reuptake inhibitor," I said. "Why hasn't anyone suggested that?"

Blake shuffled two appointment cards in his hands rhythmically.

"I don't know too much about the different chemicals," Kerry laughed. "That's for the doctor."

"The only way to deal with an unfree world," said Blake, "is to become so absolutely free that your very existence is an act of rebellion."

"Hm," said Kerry.

"I didn't say that, by the way. That's Camel Camus."

"You don't know anything about chemicals?" I said.

"The psychiatrist decides that," she said. "As well as the dosage. She's across the hall. But it's important that he sets an alarm to take his medicine."

"He's thirteen, and it's summer," I said. "That doesn't seem realistic."

"It is what it is."

I wanted to believe the solution to the problem was in that tautology, and so I stood. We would attempt to leave with the particular relief that comes after a doctor reassures us the problem is common, treatable, and will, certainly, be gone soon.

"Let me know if anything else comes up," said Kerry, looking at Blake. "Have a good one."

I took him out to an early dinner and told him he should call Deedee. He preferred not, he said. I asked about school in the fall, if he was ready for high school, I asked about girls, if he'd seen his friends lately, if he thought the salad was soggy, if he was too hot or cold, if he wanted ice in his drink, and he answered it all, monosyllabically, waiting for this, too, to be over, staring past my shoulder, watching a basketball game on TV on the restaurant wall.

On the ride back to his house, I said, "How are you feeling?"

"I don't know," he said.

"I think you do."

"That's right."

"So. Tell me."

"Have a good one," he said.

*   *   *

20

I didn't hear from Deedee or Blake for two days. I tried calling, once very late and another time early. On the third day, Deedee called.

"He really needs you. He's been asking about you."

"Is that true?" I said.

It's trite to say it: I didn't think she was proud of me. I wasn't properly pursuing my painting. Though I lied to her about it, she knew nothing was moving forward there. When she was a child she'd worked a little as an actress and a model, in a toothpaste commercial and some clothing catalogs. Then she'd danced, ballet, but was told that she wasn't good enough to continue professionally. I felt her sensing that failure in me, a lack of talent or will. Maybe she started her family early to forget dancing. At twenty came her first husband, my father, now long forgotten by her, hardly mentioned.

"Blake misses you," she said. "I'm at work, and he needs to be around people."

"What happened to his friends?"

"He doesn't tell me very much, you know I don't know. It's just how he is. But you need to go get him and take him somewhere. Maybe the mall. Only don't tell him you're taking him to the mall, or he won't go."

"The problem is he has no impulse control," I said.

Deedee used to tell me that about myself. And other things. When I was a kid, she would look for symptoms of mental illness in me—washing my hands more than I should, not eating enough, worrying excessively.

"You saying that right now doesn't help anyone," she said.

A few years ago she'd become half-aware that I had come to disrespect her, that I treated very little of what she said seriously. I'd married Victor in part because the gravity of marriage, the ritual and contract, might have distanced me from her. Of course it didn't work, and our marriage didn't, either.

I sent Blake a message on his phone: "Coming to get you. Be ready. 15 minutes."

He wrote back incongruously: "Hey qtpie."

I bought him a pizza in the mall. We ate in front of the spinning cake-like carousel, with kids on repeating horses. I took him to three clothing stores. He came out of the dressing room, the clothes too large, sleeves drooping, as if asking me not to judge him for what he was, because none of this was what he actually meant. None of it. I wanted to tell him I already knew. He combed his blond-white hair sideways like an old man, to cover a red, scabbed-over bald spot. He'd been born with it— one of those tolerable imperfections that means little at first. A salesperson suggested we try a children's store. Nothing fit.

"You shouldn't insult customers," he told me when we'd left. "Customers pay your taxes! *Imbeciles.*" He shook one fist above his head, the gesture of a cartoon villain.

I took him to a pet store. The dogs that were awake looked at us with wet, winky eyes, like beached whales barely alive. I looked back sleepily. Blake leaned on a shelf and stared. I entertained an image of us all living underwater.

"That's Leslie," said Blake, straightening his glasses. He was watching a tall, indifferent girl with crimped hair dyed lavender. She faced us and stood in front of a cage of gerbils on wheels.

"You know her from school?"

"Sort of."

"You should talk to her."

Without arguing, he did. I watched him say hello, then they stared at the cage as if at a television, saying things I couldn't hear. I walked over. She slouched, hands in pockets. I could tell she was polite, that she didn't want to be standing next to him. She seemed to be his age.

"The more gerbil pellets this guy eats," Blake was saying, "the more points he gets. Some are worth more than others, that's how the mechanism of the game works. There's an element of uncertainty. We can't know what each is worth, or even if some will hurt us."

"Gerbil food hurts gerbils?" said Leslie.

"We don't know, that's what makes us play the game."

"Oh-kaay."

"Oh-kaay," Blake repeated.

Just from her face, I knew Blake's status at his junior high school, the same one I'd gone to years earlier. He was not disliked, nor was he thought interesting or intelligent, as I thought of him, but he was simply ignored, avoided. Leslie tapped on a glass terrarium next to the gerbil cage. A pale chameleon came out from behind a vine of pale, fake flowers.

"That's Benjamin," said Blake. "That's the chameleon's name."

Leslie thumped her thumb on the glass. "I have to go find my friends," she said, though she stayed right where she was.

An elderly woman sitting behind the counter looked up from her computer. "Please don't touch," she said.

"He likes it when you do that," Blake said to Leslie. He tapped the glass quietly. "He likes girls. He really likes you. Benjamin says, 'She's pretty.' Say that, Benjamin. Can you say that? She's pretty."

"Thanks," she said to Benjamin, "but you're a lizard."

"Chameleons come from the family Chamaeleontidae."

"Oh-kaay," she said.

23

"Look out, Benjamin." Blake picked up the tiny terrarium and turned it upside down. "Earthquake, Benjamin! What are you going to do now? What are you going to do?"

He held the cage upside down, leaving Benjamin to scramble and eventually crouch on his new ceiling-turned-floor. His vine fell and landed on his triangular head. I should have stopped Blake sooner, but there's always some coarse curiosity in me that waits to see what he'll do next. Maybe he knows this.

"Young man," said the woman, coming out from behind the counter.

"Blake, that's enough," I said, taking away the terrarium.

"Young man. Young man." The woman was stunned, repeating herself, looking like a parrot with deep red eye shadow and thin, tufty black hair.

Leslie tittered. Blake smiled with his arms crossed, having won something from her, finally, a small prize he'd keep for himself.

"Is he with you?" said the parrot-woman. "I'm sorry but he needs to leave. We don't tolerate that."

I didn't apologize. I bought Benjamin and his cage for thirty-five dollars.

"I think he's starving it on purpose," Deedee said to Dullard as she set the table. "I know you think I'm crazy, but I do."

It was Saturday afternoon, and Blake had had the chameleon a week. He played with it, talked about teaching it tricks, but wouldn't feed it.

"Leave the poor kid alone," said Dullard.

"Poor kid? What poor kid?" said Deedee.

She'd been dyeing her hair blonde for years, but down one side she left a line of gray she wore like a medal.

24

"He's thirteen," Dullard said, as though explaining a wisdom tooth extraction. He had prominent ears that wiggled when he spoke. "He's a guy, and he's thirteen. Simple. That's all there is to it."

"It is what it is," I said, baiting him.

"Exactly," said Dullard. "It is what it is. Can we eat now?"

"What did he name that lizard?" said Deedee. "He refused to tell me."

I wouldn't tell her, either. Dullard's actual name was Benjamin.

Deedee liked to say the dinner table was an airplane, and all electronic devices must be turned off. Meals were for conversation. We were silent when Blake walked in.

"I was sleeping," he said. His face was round and swollen, his hair in his eyes, his scabbed bald spot exposed.

"It is what it is," I said.

"We're going to the doctor tomorrow," said Deedee. "Both of us."

"What *imbeciles*," said Blake, shaking his fist in the air. "I'm not hungry."

"Sit down. Right now. Then Miranda's taking you somewhere."

"Where?" he said.

"It's a surprise," I said.

He sat down and pretended to yawn. He quickly finger-combed and patted his hair over his bald spot. That summer I'd never seen him up before two p.m.

"I have a thought experiment for you," he said.

"Please, no," said Deedee, bringing to the table long plates of sushi rolls we'd had delivered. "Can we just eat?"

"This is important," he said. He cracked his knuckles. "You're at war."

"At war with what?" I said.

"A fictional place, okay?" said Blake. "It doesn't matter."

"Except we *are* at war," said Dullard, unwrapping chopsticks. "That's what people like to forget."

"Right," said Blake. "So pretend you're at war. You have two buttons in front of you. Two. The first saves a thousand people but all of Shakespeare gets deleted. Or Bach, or Camus, choose whoever would mean the most to you. The second button does the opposite."

"What's the opposite?" I said.

Blake placed large petals of ginger on his tongue.

"Tell us the opposite," I said.

"The second button," he said, "saves Shakespeare, but kills the people. Get it? Two buttons. The question is, how many people dying would make you choose the first button? See? It's like, how many deaths are worth deleting Shakespeare? How many people would you sacrifice?"

"Who are these people?" Dullard said.

"Not the point. It's a fictional place," said Blake.

Deedee put a whole eel roll in her mouth and chewed. "A hundred people," she said finally. "I'd only push the second button to save Shakespeare if it killed fewer than a hundred."

"Really, a hundred?" said Blake. "What do you think?" he asked me.

"I'm not sure."

"You read about this somewhere?" Dullard said. "You saw it on TV?"

"What's the point?" said Deedee.

"Just think about it," Blake said.

"Go get dressed," she said.

*　*　*

I drove us to a museum in a neighboring city, quite out of the way. The permanent collection had been donated by a mining magnate. I'd taken my adult art classes there on field trips and had gone several times on my own.

"Do you think you're a good person?" asked Blake, rolling down his window. "It's damn hot."

"I don't know," I said. "It isn't so black-and-white as that. Why are you asking?"

"I don't know." He played with a black lighter, flicking the flame, the little *flick* sounding like *kick* to me. *Kick. Kick.* "I guess I was just testing you."

"Where'd you get that? Are you smoking?"

"You ask a lot of questions," he said. "And no." *Kick. Kick.*

Visiting the museum was one of the only things I did to show I was still interested in painting, though I often claimed, to Deedee, to do much more. I'd tell her I was working when she called, but I wasn't: I'd be reading magazines or watching bad television or sleeping. I wanted her to believe something about me, that something was better now, that I was a person who did things.

There was an exhibit by a contemporary Chinese artist, Ai Weiwei, that I hadn't seen yet. It began with a photographic triptych: three gelatin silver prints of Ai nonchalantly looking at the camera, dropping a Han dynasty urn. On the floor in front of the triptych was an arrangement of ancient Han urns, similar to the one Ai dropped in the photographs, but these urns were painted in gaudy colors. *Colored Vases, 2007–2010.*

"Han dynasty," I said. "I don't know—"

"Roughly 206 BCE to 220 CE," said Blake. "I should grab one of those things and drop it!"

"Don't say that," I said. "It's like saying 'bomb' on an airplane."

"But *he's* already doing it." Blake pointed at the photos of Ai.

"That's not the point."

We passed a tour group circled around a glass case that displayed Ai's *Han Dynasty Urn with Coca-Cola Logo*. They were taking pictures with their phones; we couldn't see around them.

"Let's go," said Blake. "I feel implicated."

"Implicated? You mean complicated?"

He didn't say.

"Have you heard about Ai Weiwei before?" I said. "Some people think he's a political hero."

"Big deal," he said. "He destroys an ancient urn to say he's against destroying an ancient urn."

"Maybe it's fake," I said.

"Very original," he said.

We entered a different room, a different period, Warhol and Klee. I instructed Blake, the same as with my students at the art center. Approach carefully, stand facing head-on, and, at first, do not think.

"That's impossible, you know," he said.

I sat on a bench between two little-known Klees and started to sketch one of them as Blake approached the Warhol.

"Take a step back." A docent in a red jacket came out from his corner, making a motion with both hands. "Take a step back, son. You're too close to the painting."

"I'm not your son," said Blake.

"Just step back," I said.

He semi-stomped into the next room; I could hear him in there, walking from one side to the other, then back again,

28

flicking his lighter. *Kick, kick.* I heard someone ask, "Are you all right?"

"Have a nice day," I heard him say. *Kick, kick.*

Once Deedee asked if I loved Blake, and I told her of course, thinking it an unanswerable question, in the way most of Blake's questions were. I could not think I could not love him, and yet, between us, there existed no abstraction that could be called love. He'd have laughed at me if I'd suggested it. There were things about him I couldn't see, things he wouldn't give up.

Kick, kick. He came back into the Klee and Warhol room.

"Come here," I said. "Blake. Sit right here."

I used to rub his back when he sat next to me. He was too old for that now.

"To me," I said, looking at the Warhol, "these colors pulse, if you stare at it long enough."

He grunted and fixed his glasses on his nose.

"That's it?" I said. "You could give me more of a response."

"Well. There's just something wahoo-y about a Warhol on a white wall."

He stood and walked up to the painting as if, I thought, approaching an enemy. He was so close to it, I whimsically imagined he was seeing *into* it. The docent, who had three rooms to look after, was in the adjacent space, hands clasped behind his back, head bowed, as though he were standing in the back of a church. And Blake looked at the Warhol, as I'd told him to, but too close, peering strangely, for a long time.

I had heard there was an installation, a cube of light by Ai Weiwei on the second floor. I asked Blake to come with me, but he wouldn't move. We were there on the last day of the exhibit, my only chance to see it, so I walked upstairs. The installation was large, the size of a tiny room, a metal jungle-gym-like cubic grid, with hundreds of crystals inside, lit by bulbs arranged within it. Somehow it emotionally drained me. I walked around the cube. A couple walked around it, too, with arms around each other, and I imagined this as some kind of performance. It was a three-dimensional chandelier, a meteor of meanings, a small sun. Or else it wasn't meaningful, mere metal and lightbulbs, probably built by Ai's assistants. Children peered inside the cube with their parents. A girl reached to touch it, and her father said her name sternly, three times, until she put her hand back in her pocket.

"Will you take a picture of me with it?" A college-aged boy stood next to me with his phone.

"Sure."

"This is going to be cheesy," he said, "but it's this thing I do in front of monuments. I send the picture to my friends." He stood in front of the cube, I counted to three, and he jumped up and spread his arms out in a V. "Thanks. Do you want one of you?" he said.

I didn't, I told him. It's just metal and bulbs.

When I heard the museum alarm go off, I felt I already knew what had happened. A few other people in the cube room proceeded calmly to the exit, which is what an automated voice instructed us to do. I exited with them, but ran down the stairs, through the door to the first floor, then through to the room of Ai's ancient urns, to find Blake in the center of a small crowd, including two docents and a museum guard, their heads down, all staring at what I could not reverse or unsee—the shards of a shattered, painted Han urn. Blake looked at the shards as nonchalantly as Ai, dropping an urn, looked at us in one of the photographs.

I remember stepping over the dark pink shards and grabbing Blake's wrist. The tour group from before was taking pictures of him and the shards. I wanted to take him home, to put him in bed with soup and decide he had the flu, but four more guards arrived, and they escorted us both to the third floor. A larger crowd of people had gathered.

The museum guards took us to a small room, where two policemen were waiting with the docents and a teary museum director. The room was an office, maybe an intern's, full of art books and prints. A policeman asked Blake if he had anything in his pockets, and he surrendered his lighter and three quarters and continued sitting where they'd told him.

When Deedee arrived, she smiled bizarrely at everyone and said, "I've never been so embarrassed in all my life." I believed her.

Blake, Deedee, and I were questioned. The director didn't, perhaps couldn't, speak, except for once, to state her name for the police report, and then she put her elbows on her knees and her hands over her eyes.

It was criminal, said everyone in the room. Criminal to the police, the museum director, and Deedee for the same reasons. But if Ai-as-artist could destroy an ancient urn, how were we certain Blake-as-criminal couldn't?

I'd sometimes be convinced he held on to some precocious wisdom, but I'd also begun to think there might be *no* interior, no sketch beneath the painting, that would reveal what he was or intended to be. As easily as I could imagine his full inner life, I could imagine a cavity, hollowed out by us and all the things we'd told him he was.

"This affects your whole life," Deedee said. "This goes on your record for life."

They kept asking Blake why he'd done it, even though he appeared, as they said, "in his right mind."

"I just saved a hundred people," he said. "It is what it is."

I wanted to tell everyone sitting in that circle: we should all be blamed, it was our great burden and fault, that we were at least half the problem, but this felt glib and wrong-even-if-right—and there sat the other half, holding, in his lap, a small painted shard no one had thought to take away from him.

OLIVIA

Because I was happy, I looked for what might ruin me. I asked questions—wanting vision, prophecy—of something not there. I called it Baby. Baby, tell me what it is, I'd say. What takes this away? I meant not just happiness, but my life.

For months I was consumed by a blackish-brown screwhead-sized mole on my jaw. I delayed the appointment. I didn't want the news. The mole, I was told, was nothing. I worried about gangrene, spent hours with Internet images of dying intestine and toes. I worried for the circulation in my right leg. Down its back is a visible vein. That leg bruises easily.

I'd go into our guest room, my Asking place. Shut the door. Lie down in the impartial smell of pine and wicker. I'd say, Baby, let me be happy. Then I'd say, let her be happy. I prayed on behalf of myself.

My husband, Shannon—I want to say this—is a kind person. No other way to describe him but calm and kind; I couldn't understand. During sex I'd say to myself, Baby, let her be happy. While Shannon went down on me, I'd say it.

One April the son of high school friends of my husband's came to stay with us. Cullen was twenty-two and looking for a job in San Francisco. His father was a teacher. The mother, a biochemist for the military. Her name, that of a saint or rose, I can't remember.

We gave Cullen the guest room, my Asking place. My only Asking place; there was no other. Shannon said he'd be with us awhile but pretend he wasn't there, let him be, live a day as I would. His luggage wasn't a wheeled, rolling bag such as everyone has, but a dark, oversized suitcase, molding to green on the sides like a sea wall. I sat Cullen in front of a plate of chicken. His fingernails were smooth on top, naturally pale. I didn't know any twenty-two-year-olds; we had no children. He was blond, glowing blond like a canary, with a snub nose and a thin band of stubble beneath. Ardent and brusque and thin. He was interested mainly in some business something, to make good, good money, that was the main thing, to have his own business card, a place to wear paisley ties, he said on a third glass of scotch, and money to buy them.

"He seems quick on his feet," Shannon said later, undressing in our room. He valued wit and banter, though not in himself. And pride. We were happy together, had been for a while, but I knew about happiness and how it ends.

"Do you remember that age? Cullen's age?" I said. "Because I can't," but Shannon didn't hear me or didn't answer.

I woke early to make pancakes, ugly pancakes, put out syrup in my late mother's decanter and jars of grape and berry jams on doilies. Cullen came down the stairs in a suit, his canary hair scrunched and tangled.

"Do you need to borrow a comb?" said Shannon.

"I suppose I look like I do," Cullen said. I'd never heard someone his age use the word *suppose*.

"Do you want sausage?" I said. "Do you eat sausage? Organic sausage?"

"Oh, sure," he said, thumbing and scrolling on his smartphone. "You're a lamb."

"I'm a what?"

"You know." He looked down at his phone.

"You heard him," Shannon mouthed to me, amused. "A lamb."

Cullen licked his knife to the top and then knifed out more grape jam from the jar. I stopped myself from scolding, which I wouldn't know how to do. That would be his jar he used, only him. He scraped jam on a pancake and then licked the knife blade from bottom to tip.

"You know," he said, "that cat you've got in there's a real winner. She's a beaut."

"Cat we've got in where?" I said.

"In my room," he said, looking up. "At first she didn't like me. She was pacing around, so I called her a scaredy-you-know-what. Finally I got her to snuggle under the covers, around midnight."

"We don't have a cat," said Shannon.

"No?" said Cullen.

"No!" I said. "No cat. What are you talking about? Did you have the window open? Did a cat get in the house?"

I didn't wait and ran up to my Asking place. Clothes heaped on the bed and floor, Cullen's shirts, socks, boxers, cashmeres, and plaids. I looked into piles, under piles, the bed, the quilts and covers, in the closet, no cat. Baby, I thought, where's the cat? There were Cullen's things on the bedside table, magazines for car racing and video games, crossword puzzle books, and a thick, checked black book with a red elastic cord around it. Girls' numbers or some lines of poetry. O *Diary, I'm a naughty boy*.

"There's no cat up there," I said, coming downstairs. "I don't know what you're talking about."

Shannon blew his nose into his napkin, stalling. Then he said, "We don't own a cat. You must've had a dream. We're good at interpreting dreams if you want to tell us." It wasn't true. This was how Shannon tried to right it all.

"No?" said Cullen. "Well, she probably got out."

"Did you have the window open?" I said.

"Oh, no. It's been shut this whole time," said Cullen. "Who the Christ knows where the little lady went? She'll pop up later."

Shannon-the-Gentle kissed me a swift goodbye and said, twice, he loved me. He always said it twice in our fourteen years together, and that was how I knew he meant it. I put on a coat and sat in our yard, absorbing straight sun in a particular spot, watching a mound of decolonizing ants. What little mess and wild I could find in weeds and thorns. I toed the grass, looked up for cloud colors of near rain. No frog or bird here, no hopping thing. It was April and cold. Sun righted me. My family's company made ovens. Shannon said maybe that's why I liked the sun. How I could sit there for so long. My mother had been that way. My sister, too. We could take it. Late in the day it did rain.

The next morning, Shannon made apple batter toast with eggs. Cullen stuck his knife in the middle of the butter block, then licked the knife, then knifed the butter in mid-block again. It was his butter, I told myself, I wouldn't touch it. His to put his mouth on if you please. If I'd been younger and met him at a party, my sister and I would have called him a brute.

"How'd it go?" I said. "At the interview?"

"Oh, that," said Cullen. He had on a striped shirt almost identical to yesterday's. Someone had taught him. "The same runaround. Like I'm an imbecile. Not what we're looking for now, but we'll get back to you. That stuff."

"Well," I said. "I'm sure you were a lamb."

"Well," said Cullen, licking his goddamn knife, thinking, deciding I'd said a good thing, "I suppose I was."

I looked at Shannon. That morning I'd woken from a dream he'd gotten younger and hated the sight of me. He'd shrunk to the age of a toddler. I kissed him on the mouth and he placed his hands on my eyes and spit on me. It was the kind of dream I didn't tell. Shannon asked after Cullen's mother, whom Shannon had once idolized, but Cullen's father had won the race. Cullen shrugged and looked into his phone, a hunched creature over it, indifferent to the place.

I'd almost gotten away, about to go in my spot of sun before they could leave the table, when Cullen said, "She slept with me last night. Under the covers, again. Hey," he said to me. "What's her name?"

I sat back down. Shannon-Dear had told me if this happened, not to let anything show. Cullen was strange and tragic and a bit undone, but fine. We'd decided.

"Now, Cullen," said Shannon. "If you see a cat in your room, that's very odd. Because we don't own a cat. There is no cat in this house. This whole house." Shannon looked around the room to suggest the entirety of the house. "We would know. We live here."

"Well, she *thinks* she lives here," said Cullen. "She trots around the room like she does. And she doesn't have a name?"

"Are you listening, Cullen?" Shannon folded his hands in front of him with the calm of a sphinx. He was a lawyer for a national bank and had a way of explaining. "I swear to you. Listen here. There is no cat."

"The trouble is," said Cullen, "I never know what to call her."

They left. I went, not to my sun, that righted and clarified, but to my Asking room. I put out a foot when I opened the door, in case a cat should run out. In sunlight, on the bedside table, an empty soda can, a plastic mouth guard pitted with brown. Under the bed, in the closet, on the shelf of the closet, in a bramble of wool and tweed and ties, inside the drawers of the bedside table, between the bed and the wall, between the bedside table and the wall, beneath the chair, between the slipcover and the chair, within the sheets, no cat. There were his crossword puzzles, that thick black checked book with the cord around it; I couldn't stop. I slid the cord off. I opened the book. Five blank pages at the beginning, the silence of a dummy-dumb dolt. I closed it without looking at the rest.

Baby, I said aloud. Let me be happy. Just let me.

And, Baby, let Shannon be happy.

And, Baby, I said, before closing the door, if there's a cat in here. You show me.

I waited four seconds. I counted in my head. Shut the door. Baby, I said to myself. Let me.

Shannon phoned Cullen's parents and talked to the mother. He thrummed his top lip while he listened as if tapping out a message. Patient. He'd been a Boy Scout. "Cullen's fine," said Shannon. "Oh, yes, we expect big things for him, too. Margaret and I—yes—Margaret and I, we're so happy for you all."

"Just so you know, your son's a punk," I said over Shannon's shoulder but so Mother-Lamb wouldn't hear.

"She's getting fat," said Cullen. "She starts messing the covers up, and I can't take it. Damn cat!" He took pleasure in *damn cat.*

I'd made him get his own cereal and spoon and told him it was his spoon, only his. Let him lick.

"I have a name for her now," he said. "It's Olivia. Is that all right with everyone?" He looked at Shannon and me, as if he were beginning a board meeting. He'd chosen a sugary cereal my sister had bought with her children on their last visit. "Because, really, this is something we can decide together. I understand if you don't like it. I don't know if I like it," he said. "A lot of cats are named Olivia."

"What interviews do you have today?" said Shannon-the-Calm, Shannon-the-You-Must-Stop, unfolding the newspaper, because we believed in the importance of paper newspapers. We read the paper every morning with such contentment.

"Oh, it's at Delacroix, Lee, and Pinkle, or something like that."

"Your parents are very proud of you," said Shannon.

But Cullen was taken in by his phone, scrolling, tapping, his tongue to one side, a dark pink slug come out of his mouth, planted just above and right of the lip.

"One thing, though," said Cullen, looking up to Shannon from his phone, gesturing with his phone-scrolling finger. "I did want to mention. Olivia's been leaving little turds on the floor. I've been handling them with a tissue and hurling them out the window, but it can be a real fucking mess. They're soft turds," he said. "I'm getting worried about her. You think she's all right?"

"I appreciate that," I said.

Shannon and Cullen looked at me.

"Pardon?" said Cullen.

"I really appreciate you taking care of Olivia that way," I said. His canary hair was an avian wonder. Surely it had been dyed.

"I mean it," I said. "We've just left her in there, and sometimes I feel so terrible about it. I'm sure she needs you," I said. "I'm sure she can't wait for you to get home. I'm sure she can't wait to get under the covers."

Shannon balanced his spoon on top of his grapefruit and looked at me and brought his hands together. I worried him with my reactions. He was my lookout. We'd agreed we'd be calm. I was calm as calm as calm.

"Yeah," said Cullen, bewildered. "I'm sure."

That night he came into the living room in his velvet bathrobe tied in a true bow at his fragile waist, white cream dotting his cheeks.

"What is it?" said Shannon. We'd been watching TV.

"She's not doing so well," said Cullen.

"Oh, Jesus," I said, putting down my glass of wine.

"Olivia doesn't seem very happy," he said. "I just wanted to inform you."

"Thanks, Cullen," said Shannon. "Thank you for that."

He was like a child standing there, wanting more.

"You go to sleep," I said. "Olivia doesn't need you worrying about her."

"Yes," Cullen said. "I'll be going to bed now. Early interview." Shannon saluted him.

"He doesn't stop," I said, when Cullen was upstairs.

Later I was woken by noises at the door. Something tapped down the hall. A muted door opening, shutting. Shannon snored beside me. I'd forgotten and remembered the existence of our houseguest all in one moment. I couldn't sleep if I thought about Cullen. I soothed myself, told myself Shannon and I were alone, or as near to being alone as we could be, the thought putting me to sleep again.

"Well," said Cullen, his head down, no phone in his hand this morning. He had on an oxford blue shirt cuffed sharply. "I'm afraid I've some very bad news."

"Oh, swell," I said, putting pancakes on my plate.

"About Olivia," said Cullen. "Olivia passed away last night."

"She died?" I said.

"Yes." He was matter-of-fact, not looking at anything but his third shirt button.

"Where is she?" said Shannon.

"Well," said Cullen. "Well. I buried her."

Shannon set down his newspaper.

"You what?" said Shannon.

"I buried her, sir." It was the first time Cullen had called Shannon that. Cullen looked at me. "I buried her in the yard where I saw you sitting once, Mrs. Vaughn. I thought maybe you liked that place."

Shannon folded his newspaper in careful fours. Within it were much more terrible things in the world. "You little shit," said Shannon.

"Sir?" said Cullen, backing up.

"Don't call me that, you little fuck," said Shannon.

"Jesus Christ, Shannon!" I said.

His face was red, his jaw shaking to summon or shake the Earth. I'd never seen him that way. Never this rage. Addled by coffee, his eyelids flicked and pulsed. He rose. I rose.

"If you talk about that cat one more time—"

"Shannon, stop it! She's dead," I said. "It's over. The cat's dead."

"If you talk about that cat one more time." Shannon picked up the fork I'd set by his plate and pointed it in the air. "I'm going to take this fork and stick it up your rear," he said. His hair was caked to his forehead except for a lock in the back, vertical as a gray antenna. His face ready to burst.

"Well," said Cullen, looking at me, I believe, about to cry. "Well," he said. "Well."

I ran upstairs. I couldn't watch a word. The Asking room was neat, clothes packed and leveled in his suitcase on the bed. His crossword puzzles and black checked book on the top. His shoes on the floor. Baby, let us be happy.

Let me be happy.

Let Shannon be happy.

I looked out the window to my spot in the sun where Cullen must have seen me, where he buried the cat, he said. And let her be happy.

Let Olivia be happy. Please, Baby, let her.

QUIET! QUIET!

The daylight had stalled, as it does for children. We lay on our backs in the grass. You were counting—twenty-four thousand grass blades, you said—when the wind came, and your shirt was a sail. I'd be twelve, and you ten, by October. When I looked toward the Atchafalaya and away from you, I played a game I'd win if I held my eyes open to the sun while I said your name, and then my name. My shirt was a sail.

Melanie slept between us, straight as a snake sunning itself, her eyelids quivering. That summer she was eleven. I put some dirt in her hand.

"Stop it," you said.

"But she's dead," I said. "See?"

You had your ear to her chest. I remember her green-checked dress, your hand on her stomach.

"She'll wake up," I said. "Wake up!"

You said you didn't hear a thing, with your ear on the place her heart was, and I told you her blood had stopped, because girls don't like blood.

"Kiss me," said Melanie, with closed eyes. "Then I'll wake up and I'll kiss *you*."

"Who?" you said.

"Both of you!"

Instead I ran to the twisted tree half-dead from fire or rot and counted to a number I can't remember. Among leaves on the ground, I found a pair of lensless glasses with black, square rims, and when I came back I was wearing them.

"Look!" I said. "Who am I?"

But you were looking at two boys across the river doing cartwheels in a line in a windmill rhythm. You knelt, hands on your knees. If I had been your brother, I'd have looked like your mother, from St. Landry Parish, who had lines around her eyes as intricate as a Dürer woodcut, and who said she'd been too pretty too young too often. I would have been handsome. And I would have asked you, What is it you need?

Where are you? Not in the grass near the Atchafalaya where everyone looked. Where didn't I look? Where you are.

The boys across the river started another windmill line of cartwheels.

Melanie sat up. She was taller than both of us. "I see their peckers," she said.

"You're an asshole," I said. "An ass-lip."

"Please don't call her that," you said.

Melanie said to me, You're a stupid boy. She told me my fly was unzipped, and I checked and it wasn't. She had looked not at my fly but at my eyes. I saw you check your fly. She said she'd put pepper on us, pepper all over both our peckers.

From the road a man came with his thigh-high dog, headed toward the river. The man held a hat; the dog ate flowers and pushed its nose in the dirt. We had a game—I made my hands a cup, and you'd pour in dirt, and I'd unlace my hands until the dirt poured out a small hole at the bottom. The game was called Hourglass.

The man with the dog sat on a cleared patch of ground, and the dog ate flowers, and I got up and sat on the side of you nearest the dog, and the man talked to the dog and said hello to us, and we, not being the kind of children who'd been brought up to be more civil than necessary, said nothing. Wolf in the grass—a dog and a man with a hat in his lap—and I told you, He will go away soon, and you said, I *know*.

Melanie took a crushed pack of gum from her pocket. She put a piece in her mouth and swallowed.

"Give me a gum?" you said. And she did, so sweetly; she wanted you as hers. You were small, someone we could all agree on, vulnerable and somber. The kind of child my parents liked, in a way that made me envious, without resenting you.

The man was there, staring at nothing, his dirt-nose dog making tracks in the dirt in circles. Later I would tell the police and parents I thought it was the man who sold January fireworks, and then I took that back, because I was bad at remembering strangers' faces and their dogs, and then later, I said it was that man again. The adults didn't like this. Some of them stopped being kind to me. You should never try to unsay anything.

You wiped snot from your nose with the back of your hand and ran to the river.

"He's a baby," Melanie said, taking out a little tube of something pink to put on her lips. "What a baby-baby-baby. Oh, baby-baby-baby."

She watched me watch you.

"He could be our baby," she said.

"He's got brown hair," I said. "He looks like me, not you."

"He still could be. Baby-baby-baby."

You were taking off your shoes to shake out the sand at the river. They were cracked, with muddied soles, though your father made money.

"Want to pretend he's our baby?" She laughed. "Maybe he's like our little soft smelly baby-baby, huh?"

"Quit!" I said. I blew in her face and ran to the river. The man with the dog glanced over as if he'd been trying to sleep and we'd jolted him awake. I did as you did, feet in the water. You talked to yourself without looking at me.

Then Melanie was yelling for us. She was standing on her hands, her green-checked dress flipped in a tent over her head. "Five . . . five-and-a-dime . . . five-and-a-half . . . six . . ."

She was trying to walk on her hands—belly button, ribs like a comb, white panties with stripes. You watched. I asked you in my head to turn away. She repeated the trick. She was at the age when girls start to know they're being looked at, watching herself watching us, and that man watching her.

"Sure is interesting," you said. That was your father's inflection you were using. "Ve-ry interesting."

"Now you go, baby-baby. Your turn!" she said, coming down to the river. "Lie down. I said lie down!" and she picked up your feet and held you upside down while you stood on your hands, your shirt tumbled over your head. I tried not to stare at your upside-down body. I felt this trying-not-to shouting in my head like shouts from down inside a well.

When she let your legs go, you laughed quietly, unlike a child, maybe almost like a man remembering himself a child. You said you'd try it one more time.

It's 2017, you should be twenty-nine. Why am I remembering you this way? Why am I thinking of that town? It would be too easy to say it's because I'm depressed or regretful. When I'm waiting—in line at the drugstore, stopped in traffic in this city which I don't have the means to leave and in which I hardly live—I sometimes think of you in a place that resembles no life or afterlife. A dead body gets put away, but a missing person simultaneously exists and is lost, excluded from ordinary reality, but still part of the equation, an imaginary number. A rabbit hole.

Melanie had you by the legs, and you fell over. When you got up, you weren't standing straight.

"Do it again!" Melanie clapped her hands.

"He's tired," I said.

"You need *practice*!" she said. "I said so."

I said, Quit. She said you were learning. Quit, I said.

"Mind your own damn business," she said. You were staying on your feet, but barely. "Unless *you* want to try," she said.

I went down on the ground. I didn't want her touching me, but better me than you.

Then she had me by the ankles; up turned down. You stood on the ceiling-ground on one leg, rubbing your shin. That was when my own knee spasmed or slipped, and my foot hit her in the middle of her face, and her hands jumped to her nose. She was crying.

"He didn't mean to," you said. "It wasn't on purpose."

Blood came through the bottom of her cupped hands. I said, Sorry, Sorry. She had blood on her lips and teeth and all I could think was she looked like a boxer on TV.

"You pecker," she said.

She ran away from us and kept running until she was completely gone. Later I'd see her at school with a bandage on her face. She lived in a trailer with her grandparents. I'd never seen them. My mother says she's married now to the younger Cassidy, the homely one.

You sat near me on the grass, and I'd almost forgotten the man with the dog. The man walked the Atchafalaya's edge and pulled up his sleeves and laved his arms to his cracked elbows like a surgeon.

"Count back from a hundred," you said.

"Okay."

"And close your eyes!"

"O-kay!" I yelled.

I counted, and I would have a hundred times. I would have recited numbers backward like a madman counting seconds, looking for you.

It's 2017, you must be twenty-nine, and I want to tell you, in no true order, the things I think you've missed: New planets with new names. Earthquakes, hurricanes, tsunamis. Puberty and sex. September 2001. E-mail. Unemployment. Cell phones. Or maybe one imagines all of that, and you exist someplace more real than this. The past becomes real only if I can remember it.

I found you easily—behind the bowed, twisty tree, and you had put your arms over your head. I wasn't unselfish enough to pretend I couldn't find you, and I tapped you on the head—a little violently—and cackled in your ears. Found!

"It's not even dark," I said as we stood there. "It's not even dark and it feels dark."

"Now you count again," you said. You were angry. All I could think was that Melanie had turned you against me.

48

"It's your turn to count."

"Yours," you said.

I didn't argue. I counted back from fifty. "Come out, wherever you are!"

This time you fooled me. I looked in every place, in the patches of thickest grasses, into the branches of the oak. I thought maybe you'd gone home.

But then I heard you talking, saying, Quiet! Quiet!, and I found you behind the twisty tree as before.

When we got back to home base, our patch of grass right by the river, the man had shed his coat and squinted, as if he saw rain, and the dog was up and as glad as dogs always are. You stuck out your palm to the sky.

"Quit," I said. "There's no rain."

"*Your* turn to hide." You shut your eyes.

I walked backward.

". . . forty-seven . . . forty-six . . ."

I ran far, farther out than we'd gone before, to a monstrous tractor tire I'd seen and remembered for a hiding place. You wouldn't find me easily. I sat inside and held on and watched what light sky was left turn off. My head squeezed against the tire until my neck, so little then, fell asleep. It wasn't raining. Then it was. I watched the moon and got hungry, you didn't come, and by the time I came out of the tire to walk down the road home I was imagining our whole town eating or sleeping, shut inside, nested.

I imagine the man as a huntsman, carrying you over his shoulder. You had a mole above your right eye, and if you are not now alive, that eye is a nothing-eye, and what I can remember of you is just this sliver, a remainder divided until what's left is not enough to break.

49

CREATININE

This is about Tristan and not me. Tristan the grasshopper.

For dinner, he's laying out raw amberjack with clumps of wasabi and rice. Finger bowls of soy sauce, ginger, and, for himself, flakes of seaweed.

His movements are as precise as a casino card dealer's: he's thinking, some small admission, now to himself, soon to be spoken. Pouring our drinks—wine for him, Japanese beer for me—he talks about the monotony of buying groceries, brushing his teeth, of the ways he writes and reads; he should be traveling; not that he's bored, but he has too much to give, just stored away in him, and so he should be *somewhere*, or helping someone, helping himself.

"Maybe that sounds awful," he tells me. "Or spoiled? I think it's a privilege to casually question privilege. But I'm not spoiled."

He published a book of poems with a small press, and he started a second manuscript, even a third before the second one was finished. I told him to slow down. The first book is dedicated to his father, who hasn't contacted him in years.

"But that's complicated," I say. "You've never had to sit at a desk all day."

"Okay, but I'm here, and nothing really happens. I should *do* something, go on walks, walk in 'nature.' But in Los Angeles?" He pours tea and arranges sugar cubes in a pyramid on a plate, quick hands, like when he reads at night, turning pages with a reading writer's confident anxiety. "I could *drive* to nature, in traffic. But when do we ever do that, Pixie?"

We have what we need without spending too much, living off the money I made those years I was a paralegal. When he can, Tristan teaches. We don't have "normal jobs." Among his family, this crime is perceived to be his alone.

There's a last piece of fish on my plate. Our queen stray cat chatters in the yard; later I'll feed her in the tiny gap between our building and the next. We have two floors, a balcony—we own some large Pre-Raphaelite prints, one on almost every wall. Or maybe they're his. After six years it's hard to know. I don't like the look of sofas; we have chairs and good lamps, a table. Wood floors and almost no furniture.

He looks up from his food, and he's about to say something I've heard before. We've stopped having enough new things to say at dinner. "Gretchen says that when she had kids, she stopped having time for meals. She just eats things out of a box, she says." Gretchen is his half sister, forty-four, fifteen years older than Tristan and I. We used to see her more, before she had children. "She says when she eats, she eats—"

"Standing up," I finish. "I know."

"I tell her, 'May we all have the nerve to sit down!' " He raises his glass. "Let the word burn out on the slope of being where we are stranded." This year he's reading Yves Bonnefoy.

"It won't burn out," I say. "To wet ink!"

"To wet ink in 2055!" Tristan jabs his fork at me. "I obscenity in the milk of thy ink, Pixie!"

"I obscenity in thy mother's ink!" It's one of our jokes, a curse from Hemingway, though I couldn't tell you from where.

Tristan holds his glass over his head. "I obscenity in the cheapness of objects." He looks at our table. "And Swedish furniture stores!"

We move to the balcony. The freeway makes enough noise that we don't need steady talk. Dusk turns the brick fronts of jigsaw houses to drab bronze. Neighbors, having a party outside, dance in awkward pairs. Our drinks are full. A palm frond taps my chair in a small wind.

He's reading Bonnefoy's *On the Motion and the Immobility of Douve*. He reads to me—the poem of Douve's dark hands, and another of her dress stained "by the venom of lamps."

"The weird music starts in the hands, in the knees . . ." Douve wasn't always a woman, he says; sometimes she seems supernatural, or not supernatural, but made of Bonnefoy's wanting more than mere Earth. Is Earth mere? There is another passage about Douve in which I understand her to be waking the dead.

"Did I tell you what Gretchen told me?" he says.

"Which thing?" I say.

"That I should imagine myself as a woman. 'Fair enough,' I said, 'that's ridiculous, *I* wouldn't be I.' But I told her I understood," he says. "Male privilege. I know."

"She tells me to imagine our life with kids. All the time."

"I'm clearing out our shelves later," he says, "just what we certainly won't read."

Like Keats, who wore a suit to write, Tristan wears a sport coat. No pants, an inch of boxers extending past his coat. He's told me that if the lines do not come in one piece, they do not come. I accused him of superstition once. He admitted something to me: he doesn't like the act of writing, and he works many hours, until it exhausts him, but he likes to *have* written, the act complete, the words outside his head.

It's December, late morning. I open the curtains in the dining room, where he keeps his laptop. Rain leaks through the uncaulked windows. He sits forward, typing suddenly, the sound of solitary work, his eruptive beginnings. Speaking to himself, a sparse language. He was raised in a house in a forest, without TV. Rain like this is a stimulant—echoes from childhood, patterns in the forest, three- and four-petaled flowers, and Byzantine pathways of weeds.

We eat a long lunch. Three kinds of bread and ham and cornichons. He says nothing but is in midspeech, midverse with himself, his face like a traveler's, expecting. He told me once he thought about his quantum lives, branching from one another, and in others he wasn't a writer, though he was content and pleased, but he'd wanted this one, "Because contentment's not enough."

Our conversation consists of tasting the same food—this is my slice of pumpernickel bread, and that is yours, and both are ours. My taste in food is more conservative. If he dips his pumpernickel in his tea, he insists I try it.

After lunch, he noisily sweeps a whole shelf of books to the floor. "My exercise for today."

"Take off your jacket," I say.

He unbuttons his cuffs. "We should keep only things we truly want. We have to go through all these systematically." Sweat on his collar, he picks up his books, examining spines quickly, like a salesman or cataloger of antiques.

54

* * *

I don't remember where I went; when I return he's at the table, shirt and jacket off, his undershirt yellowed. His laptop's open. Books, all of them, are on the floor, a heap of bent or obsolete toys, some lying open. One in the middle of the pile is torn.

"I have sixty-five-year-old kidneys," he says.

"That doesn't sound like something you'd write."

He smiles and looks pained. "No. They called from the clinic. From last week." He was healthy. He had had some tests for new insurance.

"So?"

"My creatinine levels are very high. It means there's something wrong with my kidneys, very wrong."

"Too high?" I say.

"He told me on the phone. I have to take more tests, to find out what we're dealing with." He seems tired, with the remote look of when he's written nothing, or only fragments, all day.

"Call David." His cousin, a surgeon, in Maine.

"I did already, and he was very straight with me. He said kidneys filter the creatinine. If there's too much in the blood, something's wrong. I'm far above the limit, David says."

Levels like this could mean kidney failure, soon. Dialysis.

"That's not true," I say. "This isn't what happens."

"I wouldn't exaggerate," he says. "I talked to David for an hour."

I turn on all the lamps in the room.

"We should go to bed. Let's hide under the sheets and be snug-snug."

Sometimes we try to be children together—easier to repeat our made-up little chants or rhymes than to talk. He's terrified of aging, even as I watch him age. He holds up a hand to tell me to wait. His sport coat is on the floor, his cheeks are red. He says he should call his mother. That's who he can talk to. When I first met her, she kept saying she'd seen my face before. She complained of the heat and the tingling in her hands. Tristan's cheekbones, she said, he got from her brother, who, if he still lived, lived in a motel in Elyria. She quoted from Jeremiah, from Uriel in Enoch, until Tristan told her that that was enough.

"Sorry about the air-conditioning." Nathan's chopping radishes on a cutting board. He met Tristan ten years ago at Stanford, and they've been friends since—with the exception of the year after college when they didn't speak because Nathan "couldn't handle Tristan's oppressive energy," as Nathan tells it. A large potful of curry and vegetables steams on the stove. English and Spanish yells and the rushing sound of a bus come through the window in Nathan and Rebecca's kitchen.

"You're repeating yourself," says Rebecca to Nathan. "Sorry," she says to us. She's trying to be hospitable, even faintly obsequious. She's taller than I am, skinnier, and pretty in that Southern California way, some rosacea visible beneath her blonde bangs. She holds up her hair with one hand and wipes sweat from her upper lip with the other.

The kitchen's tiny, dense with scent. Their apartment is dirty and old, with stained carpet, but there are nice appliances, nicer than ours, and a few pieces of good furniture that they received as wedding gifts.

"I hope you brought onion." Nathan stops chopping, as if realizing a mistake. He nervously pushes his thin glasses up on his nose and turns to Tristan. "Wait, can you eat radish?"

"I'm going to pretend you didn't say that," Tristan says. "I'm not dying. And if I was, I'd still eat your radish."

A palm in the rain shakes in the window, the fronds like furred shoulders, epaulets. Feral green parrots live in these trees; you hear the parrots approach before you see them fly and settle in the palms in small flocks. Tristan skims his tongue over his teeth with his mouth closed: the sound of it, one of the many sounds of his idleness.

We eat a scavenger's meal of roots and leaves. I brought a twelve-dollar wine I hope is not too sour. The long, low dining table's in the living room, with their electric piano and patio chairs.

"You're lucky they're catching it early," says Nathan. "And that you have insurance. There are many things that are preventable, more and more things now. It used to be that you could die from an abscessed tooth."

"I have insurance," says Tristan. "But just the minimum."

Nathan and Rebecca write and work at day jobs, on salary. Conversations always arrive at this, especially drunken ones, which usually end with Nathan and Rebecca cursing their student loans, wishing they could live on less, and with Tristan and me in an endless loop of incredible guilt for not working a forty-hour week, for not having loans. I eat a turnip's tip and put the rest at the center of Tristan's plate. He is not eating, hasn't been since the news.

"Still, there's your father," says Nathan, "if you need him, and your sister. I just have loans. Get married. You could be on Jillian's health insurance."

"I can't put him on my insurance, even if we're married," I say.

"Nathan, stop," Rebecca says. She looks at me as though to tell me she's an ally, and she is, in a way, and also continuously kind and a little anxious.

"Hey!" Nathan, his eyes immense behind his glasses, thrusts his fork at Tristan. "I obscenity in the milk of thy kidneys, thy entropy!"

"Sold!" Tristan says, bringing down his fist too hard, bouncing the table.

Rebecca steadies her wineglass. "Jesus," she says.

"Sorry," Tristan says. "Sorry about that."

In the kitchen, I help her with coffee.

"What's he like at home?"

"Not saying anything," I say. "He gets up very early. He doesn't know how to be sick."

"He thinks he hides it." She balances cups on the corner of a card table crammed with potted dill and rosemary. She's concerned, genuinely. Although she's barely older, she has something like maternal kindness, that I both value and envy.

"Should we use this?" I point to their cappuccino maker.

"Not that I know how. We have so many useless things."

I don't want children, and she wants two, not soon—first, she's told me several times, she wants to write something significant, or at least that *she* likes, which she has not started. But there's time, she'll say, she's only thirty-three. As Tristan and I leave, she stands barefoot on the sofa, holding her ankle-length skirt above her knees, closing and latching the windows, in what must be her ritual before bed.

Our worry over the possibility of personal disaster grows in the isolation of a two-person house. Our fretting, like two notes played at once. If I try to reason with or comfort him, he won't accept. His life feels brief, he says—it's both trivial and overwhelming, not enough and too much, to want good health.

He wakes early and takes a long time deciding which book he'll read in the clinic's waiting room.

"They have no respect for your time." He picks up and puts down books from the mess he left on the floor, the pile widened and shortened. He's going to the clinic for more tests. "They think they can make you wait because they're doctors. How do I know to trust what he tells me? These are not sainted people; there's talent or no talent in doctors, too." I don't answer him when he performs his indignation: at incompetence, at mediocrity.

To tell him he is ill is to tell him he hasn't known fundamental parts of himself, or that he hasn't conceived of all branches of his quantum tree of lives. I consider making a parallel between him and sickly Keats. Rimbaud. But I remember both poets died early—Rimbaud, ill in the mountains of Harar.

Just after Tristan leaves, his half sister, Gretchen, calls. Everyone's worried about him, she says.

"And how are you? We haven't talked. Look, I couldn't get hold of him. But I'm in the neighborhood."

By the time Tristan returns, she's already sitting at our table in the dining room, fanning herself with a catalog. She's just arrived and hasn't said much to me besides Los Angeles small talk, about the traffic and heat.

"I'd hug you," she tells him. "But I'm a mess. Any news at the doctor?"

"You called her?" he says to me.

"I came on my own," she says. "What'd they say?"

"Nothing. They just took more blood." He goes into the kitchen and comes out with a tomato, eating it like an apple. "To find out specifics, to see how bad it really is."

"Why don't you come to our house tonight? Carter wants to see you. He wants you to read to him, he's been asking for you. You should be with family." She looks at me. Her floral dress is low-cut. She wears silver hoop earrings that, she's told me, people compliment her on. There's sweat on her nose and above her upper lip, and she pushes her dark hair behind her ears.

"I can't right now," he says.

"We don't have all our information, so no panicking, okay? How do you feel? Sit down."

"He's fine," I say. "He feels fine."

She watches him eat and go through the mail. He's wearing his oldest T-shirt, fraying at the bottom, and he hasn't shaved.

"I sent some e-mails to old friends," she says. "Friends from college, who are doctors."

"I'm glad worrying gives you something to do." He walks back into the kitchen. "I'm sorry, but I'm so tired."

She fans herself and looks over at me for, I think, familial female complicity, which she knows I rarely give her. From our mail, she pulls a piece of paper from a ripped envelope— one of Tristan's poems, a proof for correcting, some blue-ink markings on the typed print visible like hieroglyphs. I hear our bedroom door close. He's left me with her. Her lips and eyes move over the paper.

"I never have time to read," she says. "I haven't even read his book. I read a review of it."

"It's good," I say. "Other people say it is, too."

"You wouldn't know this, but he's just like he was in college," Gretchen says. "He knows it. He's just like that grasshopper. The ants tell him to work, to store food for the winter, but he won't because he simply doesn't want to. Now maybe he'll reevaluate things."

Her side of the family resents him. For his impracticality, they say, but really for his intensity and pride, which, though they would not say it, seem archaic.

"But he works so hard," I tell her.

"I wake up at five in the morning because I have to. He has no idea," Gretchen says to me. "You realize he'll have to take care of his mother in a few years. There's no one else to do it. Have you thought about that? She has no money. She has no friends. She has no one." Tristan's mother had been Gretchen's stepmother when she was a child, and they'd been close, Tristan had told me. But after her divorce from their father, his mother stopped talking to Gretchen. "But what I really want to know is: Is he *that* good?" She starts to fold the poem proof into fours. "I'm going to show this to someone. You don't mind? You've got to be curious, too." She unzips her purse. "I know someone who'll look at it. I've already asked them to."

"You can't take that," I say. "It's a proof."

"A what?"

"Just leave it here."

She looks up, waiting for me to qualify, to soften.

"Put it down," I say. "Put it back where it was."

I never speak to her this way—she waits for my apology.

"Maybe," she says finally, "a part of you, a small one, should be glad this is happening." She unfolds the paper from its square. "It's not life threatening. Maybe he even needs it, or you both do. Maybe he'll start to understand."

She then folds the poem into an airplane. "Weaknesses are important," she says. "I have mine; you have yours. You're more human than he is."

She says what so many already feel about him. That no one should be immune to what no one's immune to. I take the airplane away from her.

He leans over his plate. He has something to say. He is truthful—he often reveals to me what he thinks without being able to help it. The doctor will call tomorrow. Maybe Tristan won't want to tell me everything, but he will tell me. He is the only completely honest person I know, and I won't lose this.

"What happens," he says. "Tomorrow I find out my kidneys fail soon. Is that what happens? I carry my piss around in a bag, and then what?"

"But we don't know. We don't." What I do not say is that I worry the change in him will not be in one piece, that it will be gradual enough that we'll both change, mutually, without realizing. It's not that he, or we, seem more mortal, or that we've discovered mortality, but we've broken it into its phases, and I sense we have begun to enter the next phase prematurely.

In the morning, he calls the clinic and asks the receptionist for his results. He's told the doctor has them, that the doctor will get back to him.

He calls his mother. They have a way of excluding me. She spends a long time telling him what she found on the Internet: to eat juniper berry and burdock root. Water, but no wine. She tells him she prays, she hopes he feels taken care of. Once she gave me a photograph of him as a child—a cousin's birthday party, a sheet cake on a table, Tristan seated at one end, a secretive, seemingly unassailable boy on the periphery.

He sits now in his robe in front of one line on his computer screen, as if waiting for the line to multiply on its own. If it does not come in one piece, it does not come.

"I can't write anymore," he says.

"Put on your jacket," I say.

He hasn't shaved in two days, and he's eaten no breakfast. He taps the table, not the keyboard, with a kind of insect energy, steady, remote.

"We're going over there," I say. "I'm tired of this. The doctor will talk to you if you show up."

"The clinic? We might as well wait here."

"We're going over there. I'm driving."

Miles north, the Hollywood Hills houses are tiered like rows in a coliseum. I have never been this way. He found the clinic on a website, in a strip mall on Wilshire.

On the receptionist's desk, a red-lettered sign says: FULL CHECKUP FOR $95. 20 MINUTES. Someone drills in the concrete outside, and the noise shakes through the walls. A girl inconspicuously twists the dried, inky ends of her mother's hair into a braided tether. The mother pushes a banana nub into the girl's mouth, and Tristan hands me the book he brought and goes with a nurse through a door.

I read,

White under a ceiling of insects, poorly lit in profile,
Your dress stained by the venom of lamps,

Across from me a dozing man with sunburned arms has propped a toddler on the floor between his paint-spattered boots.

. . . stained by the venom of lamps,
I find you stretched out,

Your mouth higher than a river breaking far away on the earth.
Broken being the unconquerable being reassembles,

The girl sneezes banana out, into her mother's hand, waking the man, and the mother says, "All right," and the toddler begins to laugh.

Broken being the unconquerable being reassembles,
Presence seized again in the torch of cold,

The door opens,

O watcher always I find you dead,

and Tristan comes out.

Douve saying Phoenix

He gives the receptionist cash.

. . . I wake in this cold.

"I'm fine," he tells me.
"But it—"
"It happens that I'm fine."
"How can you be fine?"
"The whole first test was wrong. They tested everything this time, and everything's normal, Pixie. All the numbers are in range. Normal."
I follow him outside, into the car.
"It was wrong the first time," he says. "They made a mistake."
I don't believe him, only because it seems as though I should have foreseen it.
"The doctor seemed embarrassed; he never stopped talking."

A family of five enters the clinic as Tristan backs out of the parking lot. I wonder what they're there for. How quickly we're no longer part of the population of patients, the sick. How quickly we might be there again.

"So you're fine," I say.

"I told you, nothing happens to us," he says. "At least not now. Not yet."

"Well," I say. "And what—is there some kind of lesson here?"

"What are you talking about?" he says.

He's driving very fast. It's almost dark, car lights on the freeway, east red, west white. I imagine the grasshopper will have a large dinner and write for a while and come to bed late. He sees his life as a narrative. Sometimes a character goes through a change and doesn't learn anything, and you can't ask him to when he thinks he doesn't know how. Sometimes the grasshopper gets away. I don't know what happens after this.

Two Cats,
the Chickens,
and Trees

Dora didn't shake my hand or greet me at the door. She stayed on the piano bench at the back of the room when I entered her house. I will not come to you, either, I thought. But I did. And kissed her on her cheek. Here was a woman who looked as though she did not need me.

I'd been seeing her son for a year. She lived in a house on a mountain, a stratospheric residence from a children's book far up a spiral dirt road. Lee brought me there for Christmas when we were seniors in college. Up there, she was unknown. No friends to speak of, Lee told me, and few neighbors. Unthought of, except by Lee.

The house was unfinished, cold. The front room had a potbelly stove, a piano, a shabby old couch. Dora sat at the piano reading, her mouth moving, her eyes moving across the page slowly. Hair past her shoulders. The keyboard lid and piano lid were shut. The dog in her lap twitched and shivered, the color and size of a squirrel. Dora looked up, made a small but demonstrative noise of delight. Lee had crossed the room and bent to kiss her cheek. I kissed it, too.

"If you shall need anything while you're here," she said, "just tell me." She said *shall*. She had this other-place way of speaking, not formal exactly, not southern exactly. She wasn't southern. On the piano was a metallic sphere. Dora leaned over and touched it lightly. Thin hands, the finger bones articulated. No rings. Her fingertips lingered on the sphere, and then she left the room.

"What is that?" I said.

"The globe," said Lee. In fact, it was the size of an actual globe my own mother had kept in our living room. "We called it that for fun, but it stuck. Touch it for luck," he said, and I did. Slowly, as she had.

Lee touched the side of it. Sun through the window lit that spot. Then he lifted his hand and brought it down and pinged the globe, the noise echoing like a bell on a mountain.

"Not real luck," he said, "but you know what I mean." I didn't.

Dora offered cinnamon tea, which she made in the adjacent kitchen. Fruits and vegetables in bowls and bowls. Her celebrations required excess and feast. This was the way you lured back your wandering son. She moved between stove and countertop. Swift and sure.

"The thing with Jack is he was a sculptor," she said the next morning by the fire. "That's what he was. That's what he said when I met him. It's like someone telling you they're just about anything, and you say, okay. That's what you are."

It was early morning. I'd woken before Lee and gone into the front room. She had on no makeup but was already dressed, her long, straight hair wet. She was cross-legged on a thin bare mattress in front of the woodstove, her dog, Marina, in her lap. My mother never sat like this, would never sit on a mattress on a floor. We had a sofa and an armchair she'd bought from a catalog. We had all the things you have, in all the places those things go, when you're trying to look like everyone else.

"When'd you meet Jack?" I said.

"After Max, Lee's dad," she said. "After Max and I divorced. So this was, let's see, ten years ago. Lee was still a kid."

Holding Marina with one hand, Dora fed the fire with newspaper from a stack by the woodstove. A delicate feeding. I was in embarrassing fleece floral pajamas, my warmest. I felt my nose about to run and wiped at it with my hand.

"Jack worked with metal," she said. "All kinds of metal. He bent it. Bent it with his hands. Bent it with tools, with fire. So many burns on him from that fire. He had a little studio a few miles from his house."

On the drive up in Lee's deteriorating Jeep, he had tried to prepare me for Dora. Her ideas, what she would say. Pay attention, he'd said. She'll tell you she's making a film, but I've never seen any of it. I've never seen her working on it. Never seen a drop.

"I moved in with Jack almost immediately," said Dora. "There was rat shit in the kitchen. Food everywhere. He was just bad at things." She looked at me. "Lee isn't like that. He's lucky that way."

"So you loved him," I said. "You wanted to take care of him."

69

"Oh yes, I loved Jack," she said. "All he did was work on his sculptures every day. And I'd work on my film. I've no idea where he got money. He sold a couple, not much. We had gobs and gobs of sculptures in the house. Our own gallery, our warehouse."

"Oh," I realized, looking at the metal sphere on the piano. "The globe."

She seemed pleased I'd called it by its proper name. "Touch it. It brings strange luck," she said.

"I did that yesterday."

"Oh, I do it every day."

"I'd like to see your film," I said. "Would love to see it."

"Not yet," said Dora. "It's never done." Her dog shivered. She took the scarf from around her neck and wrapped it around the ratty thing. "One thing Jack never told me is that he had a wife. A wife, believe it? I found that out on my own."

"Mama, what are you telling her?" said Lee. He scuffed down the hall in his socks, a blanket around his shoulders. Man of the house, he'd have us believe. "Embarrassing things? You girls saying anything embarrassing about me?" He squinted into the room.

"Come by the fire," she told him. "I shall go make you tea. I waited for you."

"Tell me the story," I said. "Tell me about Jack's wife."

Lee was outside, chopping wood for the fire. He wasn't good at it, but you couldn't tell him that. Chopping gave him the temporary illusion of being self-sufficient. Dora and I were cutting apples for the salad for dinner. She'd moved the globe to the kitchen island—it was quite heavy, and I'd helped her. It should be with us, she said. She was careful setting the globe down, then touched its top. Twice. I touched it twice, too.

70

"Jack's wife," said Dora. "He'd said she was kind. I'd moved in with him by that time. This was all in Los Angeles, by the way. He'd work and I'd work and then we'd have dinner. That was our life. I had savings." She stooped and fed a piece of apple right into the mouth of her little dog. "And I see a car up the road—I was in the kitchen chopping things just like this by the window—and I see a car coming up the road, and I wonder at it. I knew when she got out of the car it was his wife. I didn't even call for him. I could tell she wasn't there to see him."

"How can you tell something like that?" I said.

"And don't you know I open the front door before she can ring the bell," she said. "She had on a suit, like she'd been to a courthouse. Well, she'd come to tell me this. She said, 'So you know, your dear one is sick.' Your dear one. Now just what in hell did that mean?"

"What did it mean?"

"He *was* sick. The disease that comes for everybody, cancer. That's what the wife ended up telling me. And then she turned around and left. Got in her car. Left."

"What was the point of that?" I said.

"Maybe revenge. Revenge on both our lives. Nothing ever in this life could—"

"Mama," said Lee, coming into the house. "Mama, where do you want me to put these gloves?"

"Nothing ever in this life could, could what?" I said.

"I'll tell you later," she said.

It's a mystery how she lives, Lee had once told me. She had some unknown income, savings, a pension from Max. When she retired from unsteady office jobs and moved to the mountain house, remoteness afforded her independence. Pride. No one there, with the exception of a few neighbors who kept to themselves, no others to exert their will, to snatch parts of her away. And there was the house to fix up, things to buy.

"You should be careful talking to her the way you are," Lee said.

We were on the pullout sofa bed in the spare room.

"Why would I be careful?" I said.

"She starts talking about everything," he said, sitting up. "She says what she wants."

"What are you talking about?"

"Just don't give in to her. She'll tell you all kinds of things. About everything."

"Listening is giving in?" I said.

"She likes to tell stories," he said. "You shouldn't listen every time."

He was taking her for granted.

"I wish my mother talked like she did," I said. My mother didn't like stories, not in books or films. Because they were untrue, she said. Because they lied. My own mother astonished me with her normalcy, the easiest thing to inherit. But I wouldn't, would not let myself.

"Let's have another walk," Dora said. "Just the three girls." Dora, Marina, me.

Christmas Eve. We'd all been on so many walks. Lee had put up a little tree by the woodstove, and we'd decorated with ornaments made from wallpaper samples and wrapping paper. We'd had cinnamon tea.

"Tell me the story about Jack," I said to her. We were going down the mountain with Marina on her leash. Dora had on earrings she'd made from wallpaper. She used to sell her wallpaper earrings at farmers' markets. "Tell me what you said last time. About revenge. Nothing ever in this life could what?"

"Honey, I don't remember what I was trying to say," said Dora. "But Jack. Jack was sick. Verifiably sick. He wouldn't let anyone touch him. He wouldn't let any doctor touch him, and no nurse in the house with him. Not that we could afford one. So he kept bending metal the way he was."

"For his sculptures."

"His sculptures," she said.

"The globe," I said.

"Yes, the globe." She sighed.

"And then what?" I said.

"And then one day we couldn't afford his studio. And we had no room in the house. We got a storage area. We rented one. And we packed all his sculptures and we put them in there. But nothing ever in our lives could stop us from making things. He started bending metal at home and making things and putting them in the rented place."

"You can't be stopped," I said.

"No," she said. "Some of us can't. We just go forward like nothing ever. Some of us do. Like with my film. I never stop with it."

"I know you don't," I said.

"It's how you make anything. Something from nothing."

We were coming up to the house again, the yard: chickens in a wire enclosure, two cats sleeping beneath jasmine and spearmint, planted fruit trees. A dishwasher on its side, a bicycle. She patted each cat on the head as we passed. I petted the smaller one, the female.

"You keep forward. Nothing ever in your life," she said, "keeps you from it. Tell me," she said, "you understand."

I said, "I understand."

And I did.

"Jack died," said Dora. "It was very drawn out. It was terrible. I made him have a doctor at the end, at the house. The doctor was a friend and didn't charge. Jack was on meds, lots of them." Marina stopped and shook herself on the leash, then started walking again. "Nothing ever in this life should be that," said Dora. "It's so hard waiting for it and delaying your grief. I can't tell you. You feel like a jellyfish."

"You felt like a jellyfish?" I said.

"I don't know what I'm saying."

"Yes, you do."

"I miss work," she said. "I miss the film. It's really coming along, but I need to work more."

Her quiet life, the sphere of cold metal. I imagined her, resident of that globe, playing piano on a metal planet.

"You've got to stop," Lee whispered, when we were back in the spare room. "You've got to stop letting her take you in."

"She's not taking me in," I said.

"Don't get so excited," he said. "I know how you think of her, what you want from her."

"That's because you already have it. Can't I want a thing? Or wish it?"

"Pay attention," he said.

She was right by our window, talking to her animals. I could hear the chickens beating wings, and I thought something I haven't repeated—I wished to live with Dora and work for her and feed the chickens, the cats. The dog barked right then.

"Oh, Marina," I said. "That dog." I said it, trying it out, as if she were mine.

"That isn't her real name," said Lee. "That's not the name we gave her."

"What is it?" I said.

"I don't remember."

"Yes, you do."

He looked at me.

"You don't have to tell me," I said. "I'll ask Dora."

It was Christmas. Colder in the house than ever, blankets around us, sitting on the mattress in front of the woodstove, unwrapping a book from Lee, a necklace, boxes of tea from Dora, a lace scarf from Lee for Dora, Marina playing in the red cellophane. Jack's globe on the piano. I gave Dora a candle. She lit it immediately, and I wanted her to save it. I wanted her to wait until it was the two of us.

Lee went into the kitchen. Dora pulled her dog into her lap and kissed her on both eyes and swaddled her tightly in her scarf. She looked at me.

"Ask me what happened," she whispered. "That's not the end."

"What happened?" I said.

"And then," she said.

"Yes?"

"And then I buried him. His wife even came to the cemetery. The day we buried him I went back to the storage room to see our things. Nothing ever in this life could keep me from that." She looked around. "And I've got to tell you this. The storage place had filed for bankruptcy. That's what they told me at the front desk. And you know what they did? I'm serious now. You know what they did?"

"Tell me," I said.

"They'd gone into our storage room and someone had scrapped all the metal."

"Please," I said.

"No, they did, they'd taken it all away," she said. "There I was in a black dress, a widow."

Lee had come into the room with an open package of cookies.

"I almost don't believe it," I said.

"What happened?" said Lee.

"That would be your choice," Dora said to me. "You believe what you have the will to believe."

"They took everything?" I said.

"Oh, everything. Everything. I swear to you, Emily. I couldn't believe it."

"I'm so sorry," I said.

I started to stand and go to her but stopped myself.

"I couldn't believe it," she said.

"Oh," said Lee. "I know the story she's telling. It's the sad one about her aunt."

"No." I looked at him. "Jack."

"Oh," he said, chewing a cookie irreverently but touching the globe gently. "Of course. Jack."

"Oh, poor us," she said, watching him. "Nothing ever was like that."

She was crying now.

"Poor us," I said. I was starting to feel sick. I cried instead.

"I couldn't believe it," she said to me.

We were just crying. Crying what we could.

"Poor us," she said. "Poor all of us." She looked at Lee. "Poor everything all of us. Poor everything everything all of us. Everything everything poor poor never not never everything."

Lee went to her, put an arm around her, still chewing his cookie. She laid her head on her son's shoulder. She swaddled Marina tightly in the blanket.

"I told you," he said. "She starts talking about all of it. Everything, everybody."

"It is about everybody," Dora said.

Lee hugged her. Told her nice things, and she smiled at him and kissed Marina on the head. Kissed Marina again. They had what they needed. Nothing from me.

This is how you love a mother: you resent her. You lightly scold her when you believe she's comically quaint or false. Her tasks and complaints, you must look after. Similarities between you should flatter and frustrate. You must never admire her without wishing to be unlike her. You must hate when someone else loves her.

THINGS THAT AREN'T THE WORLD

Dear Stell,

Kim Il-Sung, our dear fish, is dead. Mother says you've been very unhappy lately, and only an idiot would tell you that the dying fish (hundreds of miles away) somehow knew. Nevertheless, my roommates and I (you've met one of them, the one with the, as you say, cavern nostrils), we were all very worried when Kim migrated to the bottom of the bowl and would not get up, not even when I read to him from my Tremendous Textbook regarding recent earthly ills, such as the problems of storing coal slurry. He lay there, but alive, for two days, and I sang to him Battle Hymn and Wenceslas, the way you used to like, groaning in bed when you were a kid with some mumpy lumpy head cold. Then Kim's end came—it must have happened at night, since I only noticed the very hung morning over after. So I fittingly buried him in the miniature flowerpot you bought and painted and left here by mistake. That was during your visit, when you bought Kim Il-Sung, Eternal President of the Republic, just a wee sperm of a goldfish then. Mother says you've been unhappy a long while and do not leave bed. This happens to fish, too.

My roommates—do you know what they do while I write this? They play elaborate video games that tell them they're combat soldiers. Graham, for example. Graham is only five foot four, but here in our living room he believes he's an expert at shooting foreign enemies from a tank. Maybe he *is* killing them, real men, somewhere, by remote, and I sit watching him on our crusty plaid couch in my underwear drinking milk and eating a sliced orange. Graham is one of those "guys" who've been plunked down in the middle of the universe without any knowledge or concern as to any historical fact of, or before, their own existence. In other words, to him the origin of the egg is the frying pan. And so, my egg, please write.

Fin.

Finn—

This is a problem you should take seriously.
Here's a quick summary:

She's been in bed a week now—she won't come
out . . . I have no idea what's going on.

I asked her if it has something to do with a boy but I
know it doesn't.
I was up with her all last night as she recounted a bad
dream . . . something to do with an eclipse turning us
into polyurethane.
I saw her early this morning and she was still sleeping.

Unless you have anything *nice* to say to her, pls say
nothing . . . I wish you'd help—she's supposed to go back
to school soon, etc. I don't even know what time it is.
Gd night,
M.

finn-fish,

it isn't funny. it isn't funny at all.

stella
ps: i didn't like kim.

Stella and Finn—

Don't worry . . . Stella, don't worry. What you're
going through is perfectly natural. It's a problem, like
anything else.
Here's a good example:

I have a thyroid problem. My thyroid produces too
much hormone, and I take pills for it every day . . . I'm
saying I take pills for a problem, and it's okay. Neither
of you has said to me, Mother, Stop taking those pills.
Never. You wouldn't want me to. You need to be
thinking about this, about the possibility—

We'll talk later bc I'm e-mailing from work . . . I
have patients, patients who have heart problems or
stomach or liver, and they acknowledge that and take
action.

Lv.
M.

dear Finn and Mother,

dear Finn, dear Mother.

your stell

Dear Stell,

Mother says you haven't left your room. It's a perfect middle-class privilege to be staying inside all day,
the way you do. (It's a perfect middle-class privilege
to go to college, the way *I* do.) And what do you *do*
exactly? Eat and sleep, like a good middle-class girl
waiting for (ah!) *something else.*

I know you enough to make guesses—guesses
much closer than Mother can make—about what's
been wrong for so long. Last Christmas (christ what a
ridiculous christmas of a christmas), I already saw this
happening. I saw you feared where you live, in Mother's little nesty house that looks like all the nesty-rest
on the block. I saw you feared what you think you'll
become. You even told me you feared your choice
for college, *feared a choice already made.* And now
you won't leave your canopied bed. Is it that you, at
the post-sweet age of seventeen, fear granite countertops and flat-screen televisions and walk-in closets
and stainless steel appliances? Maybe, in a few years,
you fear you will meet a nice young man—perhaps
a computer programmer, a teacher or lawyer (by the
way, I tolerate any of these)—and you'll have some
job somewhere, or not, and there you'll be (living in
that same town where you and I grew as much as
we could), cleaning your granite countertops with
cleaning spray (bought for seven dollars out of your
joint checking account). You'll post pictures on the
Internet—pictures of yourself, your home, your salty-
Thursday-afternoon margaritas on your umbrellaed

porch. Pictures designed to garner praise, affirmation. (But, Stelly, you'll have central air-conditioning in your starter home! I have only this little fan on my desk that dries out my eyes.) Maybe you'll be so far gone as to put up photos of your children toilet training. (Unthinkable!) What will you do with yourself? Many children? A dog? Watch television? Have a happy hour date with the girls from work? What work? Train for half-marathons? Remodel the house? Do you fear this?

You fear your choices have been made. You think you're a buoy that goes where the water takes you, and you are not wrong to think it. I am that, too. But I have distractions—namely, this damned education I'm after, and, yes, girls, girls, girls—but, Stelly, these are merely places in the water that keep calm enough, places where I can rest. And then the waves come again, and the buoy (myself, a speck) goes where it will.

I still see you as a child, which isn't fair to us. You told me those creatures, those things with the turtle-like shells, the Reebles, you named them, were alive in the hedges. They're poisonous, you said. You were afraid of them.

If I had you here now, I would tell you about this ancient culture I'm reading about. They must take care of providing food and shelter for their children. I think they've established an order to things.

Fin.

Dear Finn—

Pls let me handle your sister—she shared your
e-mail—I've always respected and loved your
extremely rare bird brain, but you aren't helping. You
should remember that many meals you've enjoyed
in my house were cooked on those bourgeois granite
counters which you so heartily despise—
    when's the next time you're coming home?

Lv.
M.

dear mother and finn-fish,

i am writing you now i want to at the moment and
that is all. i watched a bumblebee outside my window
just now and all i wanted was for Bee to stay. it was
black completely and buzzing THROUGH to me
and are these black bees the kind of bees that sting? i
don't know who knows (YOU would, finn) . . . and i
worried. it flew in then out, then worried, then darted
at a little hole by my window maybe it thought the
hole was a hive. but then (SILLY BEE!) thought better
of the whole thing and flew away, and i didn't think
about IT anymore. how many minutes was that?
maybe that bee being here was five minutes. a thing
that took up five minutes of my life.

stell

Dear, dear Stella,

I'm writing you from work bc you won't listen to
me . . . you won't pick up the phone . . .

When I left this morning, you'd eaten nothing and
were pretending to sleep. I knew you weren't sleeping . . . your poor mother is much more aware than
you think—

You've been in bed 10 days, and I've let you have
your time, but that's enough . . . I've seen various
changes in you for months . . . many changes, gradu-
ally, and so has Finn. I want you to see someone, a
psychiatrist, a friend of mine . . . I really think you
should talk to someone who's trained in addressing
your symptoms . . .

Second, you should know that there are many
different kinds of medications that may help. I'll
never push anything on you—you know that—but
in the same way I take medication for my thyroid,
medication in your case might help. For example,
there's fluoxetine, a serotonin reuptake inhibitor, it's
extremely popular and effective someone told me.
There's also sertraline . . . and other things . . . point
being, there are options, and these are just kinds of
treatment, Stella. We'll talk about this later. Don't
worry—I'll call you after 4:15—
Lv.
M.

Dear Finn,

Update on your sister. She couldn't sleep again and
then finally she slept a little and so I did. Then she
woke suddenly with one of those dreams . . . where
does a seventeen-year-old get these images? In this
dream there was plastic again . . . and she said she was
salt in the dream and that a strange man was throwing her, just some white salt, against the bottom of a
plastic tree.

She asked me, What's the purpose of my life? I
said, to be a good person, a good citizen . . . Which
you are, I added. And you can do or be whatever you
want to be. You're seventeen—

I wanted you to know that all of this is going on—
I'm at work. I know you're busy and work hard.

Lv your M.

BEE is not back. i admit i thought maybe it would come. probably it won't at all. because it's very tired and truly because it doesn't want to go anywhere. not at least anywhere in the world.

stell

Mother!

You "mean well" (I know). But please don't increase her sense of young ego and entitlement with mere clichés. (And don't get upset with me for saying that! You know I'm right. Do not write to me until you think about this a little bit, please?) You know what they say about our generation. I see all that mad hormone and bullish, bully ego and entitlement at this fine institution I attend. And for what? These twenty-year-old college juniors think they can "be whatever they want to be" (merely because they are human)? Because they live and breathe and have lots of sex and drink beer and eat cheez doodles—this makes them special children???? Please, Mother, stop filling her head with it.

Your Loving Finn Who Wants Only Good
(But Not Simple) Things

Dear my well-intentioned Finn,

I'm not responding to all this yet. In the meantime—
please don't forget to use condoms—

M.

BEE is back! right now and i wanted to tell you this while it is happening. i hope you are reading this at this SECOND wherever you are, office or school. write back to tell me if you are and just think THIS is a minute of your life thinking about a bee. THIS.

stell

Stella,

I'm bw patients right now but pls promise me you're eating something.

M.

Hi, Bee.

Finn here. And wherefore do you sting?

because i have no other life and know no other thing.

Bzz, Bee

Dear Stellest of Stells,

I'm in lecture, crammed between two sleepy, drooling freshmen in sweatpants! (Have you noticed these sweatpants girls wear with words on the rear? I HAVE.) We're being told there are metaphors everywhere, in the strangest of places, but you know all this already, somewhere in your head, which, less and less alas, is my head.

Mother told me you asked her an important question. Good, ask questions, as long as you remember that you are generally not the first to ask them. Yesterday I read a poet who says you must name the world. By that I think he meant not just what you see but what you don't. What you know and don't really know. But we're all so tired. A little bit hungover from nothingness. I'm tired of looking at my laptop and phone. We're all tired from things we can't really name, or things that don't deserve to have names. And these things that aren't the world.

The purpose of your life is to walk out of your bedroom, out of our house, and into the sun and into the yard, and to find your little creatures in their shells, your Reebles, in the hedges. And don't let them poison you.

Fin.

Finn, call me . . . I'm at work but I'll answr. M

Why aren't you picking up your phone—Stella just
left me a message saying she was going to your
father's, which I don't believe . . . she claims she's
taking a cab, but that's 40 miles . . . when was the
last time she was there? A year ago? I phoned yr
father and he confirmed she's going there but I can't
trust what he says and I've tried calling her many
times . . . the phone doesn't even ring . . . there's
nothing on the other end and I don't know—call me
as soon as you get this and call yr father for me. I
don't believe anything he says.

Stell?

Please answer your Fin-Fish.
(Please.)
StellStellStellStellStellStellStellStellStell, answer your Fin.

Fin.

Mother,

You need to calm down. I believe her that she's gone to Papa's. Nothing happens when I call her, either, but I believe her. Just calm down. She's an adult, practically.

Finn

Stell?

Fin-Fish needs an answer. Call or write your Fish.
(And you've got people worried. Mother is worried.)

Love,
Fin.

Finn,

It is not your place right now to tell me when to
calm down . . . did you talk to your father? It doesn't
matter. He's completely untrustworthy . . . but that's
because he has his own trust issues—you know that. I
need to know where she is.

Stella,

Pls answer your mother. We need to talk very seriously. I need to know where you are. One day you will have a daughter and understand. Please.

Lv. your M. who needs to hear from you right now

Stell,

I've driven the 500 miles to Papa's place and of course you're not here. And he's lying to Mother for you because he loves lying to her. This isn't funny now. I've driven all the way out. I've left school. I'm missing classes. Here I am. Where are you?

Fin-Fish

Stell, Stell, Stell,

You won't answer me?
Where are you?
Where are you?
Where are you?
If I ask you three times, you'll come out?

Fin.

fish,

here i am.

Mother,

She's all right. She's fine. Stop worrying.

Finn

Where are you, Stell? I don't like you by yourself. Tell me where you are, and I'll come. Fin.

fin-fish,

i went out on the street this morning fin-fish and got groceries. i was walking out with my bags and there were so many people and NOT ONE SQUARE-INCH without people in it like a ZOO or amusement park. i could barely see ahead of me anywhere and then i looked down. there was something beneath everyone's feet. many things. like soft bodies left over from the shells, and there they were, all of THEM, the Reebles, not dead or alive and still and lying like that in the street without their shells. and without their shells, well. without them i knew i was wrong. they WEREN'T poisonous. they felt safe. of course i was not afraid.

you don't have to believe me, i don't believe it and i saw it. or i didn't see it, but i imagined i could and that's what you asked me to do without asking. the point is i can see them when i want to and know they are both there and not there, and somehow that makes me sane or saner than most people and maybe even mother could understand and papa could. and yes YOU always can.

i'm a spoiled girl who knows nothing and says the wrong words. i'm selfish but feel sick and then feel guilty for it. you have an idea of what i mean. so i had to be away from people, people who know me.

Stell

Where are you, Stell? Tell Fin?

i've found my own shell! and am just fine, my fish. it doesn't have very much except for a bed and towels and desk. it's a small shell for a bee named Ree. it costs a little money that i already have. i have a way of doing things.

i wish you had some such Reeble-shell as i have, my fin. i imagine you here.

Stell,

I believe you. I will talk to Mother. She's worried, of course. You understand. But basically, don't worry.

For now, stay in your Stell-shell. I know you need to, but . . . it isn't all right for you to leave everything and lock yourself up for more than a while.

Today I came down from Papa's mountain and went to the city. I looked at the sidewalk below everyone's feet—a place no one else looked—and if I squinted I could see THEM on the pavement there sort of breathing beneath everyone. No one looked at me looking. It was like people had no faces.

Shell yourself away, for a while. Shell everything away right now, and let nothing in. Then tell me where you are, and I'll come get you. Because you can't truly be alive alone. This can't be your exit.

Fin.

PITTSBURGH IN COPENHAGEN

There was a great tenderness to the sadness when he would go there. She knew how much he loved his wife. They were like casualties helping each other as they waited for the end. She cooked their dinner at the stove, her blonde, bent head reflected, like an abstract sun, in a stainless steel pan on a hook.

On the table, delftware bowls of eggplant and sausage. Cricket on the English-language station on the radio. She didn't like to talk at dinner—her English could be difficult. He brought out lemon and onion and folded the paper napkins the way she liked. She insisted on serving him. Or, if not casualties, they were thieves, taking these afternoons and evenings for themselves, their appetites, gathering up the few coins that had spilled in the act.

He got up from the table to get the child, her son, who'd woken and started to call. Beneath the mobile of rotating planets and stars at the foot of the crib, he found the child on its stomach, trying to hold up its head, its neck stretched like that of a straining tortoise—it could not make itself go where it wanted. In the crib was a small machine, simulating sounds of the ocean. *You strange island*, thought the man. *Little life.*

At the table, he held the child facing forward in his lap, so that it leaned toward its mother and the half-finished dinner into which she'd put so much effort. The man offered her a sip of beer, and she refused. There was something withheld about her now, eating very little very quickly. He supposed he liked to watch her eat; she almost revealed herself that way. One-handed, he tore a chunk from the top of his buttered bread and rolled it in a dense small ball between his fingers and offered this to the child—it was crying again, twisting its torso, coaxing itself into a fit.

"Give him to me," she said.

"It's all right." The man tried to comfort the child, rubbing its heel between his fingers. A plain smoothness.

"I can take him." She held out her arms.

"Just eat," he said. "Relax."

But she said she was finished and scraped flecks of salt and garlic off the table with the edge of her hand into her napkin. He felt his beard for crumbs and decided to tell a lie—that this had been his favorite meal. Maybe what she gave away to him was in her face, in the particular immobile expression that asked him to spend the night when she already knew he would. What she knew of his wife in America was all he'd told her—married fifteen years, almost.

The child had now screamed for what seemed like a minute, as if without taking a breath. The man turned it around in his lap. He held it by its fragile chest.

"Are you ready?" He pushed back his chair.

He threw the child up, nearly two feet above the tabletop, then caught the child. Very easy. It had stopped crying somewhere on the way down.

"I prefer you do not do that," she said calmly. "Before I said that."

She cleared the table, leaving his unfinished plate. She swept the kitchen while the child, quieted, kicked its legs in the man's lap. He consoled it, patting its back, whispering to it what Danish he knew, simple phrases. *My dear. You look beautiful. Two coffees, please. Down the hall, to the right, second door on the left. Mr. Iversen doesn't work here anymore.* He put his pinky in its mouth and felt the tiny tongue. He tapped the tongue, softly. She'd named the child after its father, who worked in the Faroe Islands eight months a year. It was just learning to turn toward its name, which she sang a few times as she swept.

He sat with her son whimpering in his lap for a long time, longer than he preferred, listening to it ask for what it couldn't say. With the radio on and the white noise of water running, the whimpers churned his thoughts. She put on an apron and blue rubber gloves and washed the dishes.

"Do something for him?"

She turned her English sentences to questions frequently. Within her was a detailed life in a country still mostly unknown to him. Her mother had died before he'd met her. She'd been married to the child's father and then divorced, and the child had come after. One life alongside hers, then another. *And now me*, the man thought, *and soon not*.

She held a dish to the light. "What is this? Water streak?"

He'd taught her that last word, and she'd been sure to use it every day he saw her; each time, it seemed to lose part of its definition. *Rain streak. Streak of pepper, streak of skin.* Once, after he had given her a short lesson, she told him she laved him.

He walked out of the kitchen and around the apartment, the child still kicking in his arms. She kept almost nothing in those rooms. In her bedroom was a hooked Armenian rug he'd bought for her at a shop two months before. She'd strung silver lights through the fretwork of her bamboo bed's headboard. He could feel himself hoarding images to remember later. On her dresser were lipsticks next to a bottle of perfume the color of brandy—he saw his person in the mirror, holding this woman's child, a woman who had hardly any family photographs, who preferred rugs and dishes to jewelry, who had asked him so little about himself because she knew they both preferred it that way.

The phone rang. Four times before she answered, then laughter and—from what he could tell, from the English nouns among the Danish—she talked about an old American movie. He'd seen it in Pittsburgh. He was fourteen in a Cineplex with a marquee, and with a girl from school who'd kept her high heels in a box hidden in the bushes in her parents' front yard. Now in the mirror, he held *this*, this woman's thick-legged son.

"Comrade," he said. "You have to stop crying."

In Pittsburgh, his father had had factory work. They'd lived in a small house, he in one bedroom with his brothers. His mother had put lamps everywhere, candles. The bill wasn't paid. She decorated the walls with blank postcards of foreign cities. He remembered it all. He was almost ashamed for his great happiness in that plain life.

She hung up the phone and turned off the radio, but immediately turned it back on for the news. Something about an important election.

"Enough," he said to the child. "You're fine now."

The phone rang again. She picked it up before it could ring twice. She never received phone calls when he visited, and tonight there had been two. He went to the archway in the hall but still couldn't hear her above the radio.

With the child, he walked to the kitchen door—her head was down, her hand cupped over her mouth and the mouthpiece, a rubber glove tucked in her armpit, the phone cord stretched to the far side of the room. The sink water ran. He watched her.

She was at the kitchen window, opened out onto the shared courtyard where he had installed a small swing after the landlord and neighbors had agreed to it. She'd begun to talk loudly. So much of her life he could not account for—she contained too many decoys, invisibilities, trapdoors with latches easily triggered. She held the phone away from her, as if holding something infectious. Then suddenly she yanked it back, jerking the cord, yelling into the mouthpiece in Danish, she was tired, fuck, *lort*—this word he knew—and hung up. She went to the sink, turning the water off, then on again. He walked into the room with her quieted son. She didn't turn around.

"What does he need?" she said, scratching at food on a plate with a fingernail.

"Who was it on the phone?" he said.

"He needs diaper."

"*Sig det,*" he said. "Who was it?"

She looked at him with the water running. "I am not yours. You are not mine."

"Nevertheless, you can tell me."

"Doesn't matter, I said."

In the child's room he turned on the tiny television for sports, anything. *The man changes the cloth diaper of her child.*

119

This stranger in front of you, holding you. He almost didn't know if these were thoughts or if he said them aloud, but he observed himself, the evening. *The man changes the baby in the woman's apartment. She knows what he almost knows, that he will leave after tomorrow. Not leave, stop coming.*

"You see? Powder. Under your legs." He held up the powder. "What fine, fat legs you have! Fat, fat! And now the diaper. Clip, clip. Now we tuck in the cloth." He surprised himself and sang, "Clip-clip, and tuck. Fat, fat legs, clip, clip, and tuck."

He snapped the bottom of its pajamas.

"You have nothing to say?"

The child sucked the back of its hand and looked at him, focusing. *Nothing?*

"Must be the world is at peace," he said.

In one of the few photos in the apartment, above the crib, she had her back to him sitting on a towel on a pebbly beach. Another woman, her sister, stood above. He'd met the sister once, accidentally, when he'd shown up at the apartment on the way to his office at the embassy. The sister had been visiting. She hadn't introduced them, but had curtly kissed her sister before seeing her out. When the door closed, she told him—afforded him—the thoughts on her face: *please, never uninvited.*

How directly had he ever looked at her? She was remote and posed, sometimes even in bed. She frustrated people, she had told him with a little satisfaction. She required one's patience. Her emotions were practiced, harbored, or unresolved.

"Are you ready, Comrade?"

He lifted the child and anchored his thumbs in the small and satisfying cushions of fat in its armpits, tightened his fingers on its shoulders. *The man, getting older, straightens his back. He throws the child in the air.* He threw the child up again, higher, or high enough, that it might feel an envied weightlessness.

"Pittsburgh."

He threw the child again. This time he waited until it reached his chest to catch it.

"Pittsburgh," he said into the child's ear. A word the child would never go to. "Pittsburgh."

He threw it up with some force, and it smiled with prearticulate glee at the man, who was leaving the child with a trace of himself.

They were in bed, not sleeping or talking, listening to more of the evening news, when the doorbell rang. They'd gotten the child to sleep around seven.

"What now?" he said.

"No idea," she said.

He'd propped a small heater next to the bed. They were drowsy, shirtless in their jeans—he feared any ritual tonight, including sex, and he told himself he was right in guessing she did, too. Maybe he wanted to feel sorry for her, and could not—could never, she was too good for that—and he showed it. Sometimes that was his mistake, revealing some negative thought, then acknowledging his misstep with a weary remark or inflection. She could extract those confessions without effort, without a word, or, worse than that, she might make him think he had something to confess. *But nothing.*

"Who is that?" he said. "Everyone's calling you. The baby will wake up."

"Check on him," she said.

"It's very late." He was putting on his sweatshirt backward. "*I* will get the door."

"You think this late?" She buttoned her shirt, moving her long hair in front of one shoulder. "Check the baby? You, please."

It was asleep, with the balding stuffed animal, a large parrot, pinned beneath it. She'd put on Mahler—someone had told her that would be healthy, good for the child's brain.

He closed the door and listened from the hallway—she was laughing, talking unlike herself, a high-pitched and courteous tone. He went to the front door to see a man in a fleece vest and coat with a clipboard held toward her, which she leaned over, keeping her hair out of the way. On the table was a white vase of red tulips.

"Who sent tulips?" he said.

"No card." She went to the table to smell the tulips, one of them batting against her nose as she inhaled.

"Nothing?"

"No. I think they are for Christmas. But who has tulips in winter?"

He looked at the deliveryman and pointed to the tulips. "*Fra hvem*? Can I see?" He took the clipboard from the deliveryman. Almost nothing on the paper—just her signature: something, he realized, he'd not seen before. It was strangely precise and legible.

"Wait," he said. "These aren't ours. Two-B is across the courtyard."

"*Hvad?*"

"It's the wrong apartment."

"No, let me see." She went to her purse on the table by the door and pulled out a pair of glasses.

"Right here, see?"

She held the glasses in front of her face and read the

clipboard. She spoke to the deliveryman in Danish and re-turned the flowers with a shrug and then laughed after she closed the door after him, a performative laugh, maybe out of embarrassment. But then he watched her transition, as if coming back to her life—only for a second—composing her face, lowering her voice.

"The baby's asleep?" she said to him. "He needs me now?"

"No, he's asleep."

"Wait," she said, swatting the air with her hand and putting her ear toward the hall. "Did you hear that?"

"There's nothing. I said he's asleep."

"Thank the god."

"You thought those flowers were for you?"

"I wouldn't know."

She walked to the other end of the room, to the grandfather clock they could never get to work.

"*Kære*," he said. "Who did you think they were from?"

"What?"

"I'm asking you a question," he said.

"I can never tell you what you want to say," she said.

From her face he knew he'd given something away. She stood there, maybe holding whatever he'd given her, maybe anticipating something else—a thing he might say, the child, the phone—wanting a thing to distract them again, to intercede. She didn't know what that was, though she waited for what might relieve her, what would not refuse her.

RUSALKA'S
LONG LEGS

We buried my great-great-grandmother in 1990 with a diamond royal flush in her hand. She played poker twice a week at the casino in Lafayette. She had friends and cancer and debt. Her face was thin, mottled. She had arthritic knees, atrophied legs like a doll's. At home, she was almost always in a chair or bed.

Her house—heirlooms and cats and photographs of ancestors, our ancestors padlocked in a concrete tomb in the graveyard five miles away. The oldest family member alive, she said, is the one who lives with the dead.

What Ula said I believed. She could not walk from six to nine.

Her legs. In 1908, outside New Orleans, she was six and following her mother, Del, up a hill. Del was ahead, her blonde-white hair in rough straight strands so dense that if Ula had drawn her hands through that hair, if she'd covered her face with it, she told me she'd never have found her way out.

You like it here, walking with me? said Del.

Yes, ma'am, said Ula.

How long would you walk? How far those little legs go?

Far as I want.

Ula wore a little dress and, in her hair, a barrette she would later lose. They were walking through sparse woods on a hill behind a hospital, Our Lady of Lourdes. Del had a room in the ladies' ward, fifth floor. Ula's father had dropped Ula off for a full-day visit, and Del had introduced her to all the nurses, some of the patients, but none of them, thought Ula, looked sick. She had sat on the sunporch while it rained, sucking a garlic clove the hospital cook had given her. When the rain had stopped, she and Del went to the hospital rose garden and chased a glossy black bee, and the nurse wasn't looking, and Del picked Ula up under her arms and lifted her over the fence. Then Del herself climbed over.

We're rabbits, you and me, Del said, taking Ula's hand. Rabbits who only go uphill. And they don't stop until a hundred trees later.

Is Clark at the top? said Ula.

I'm not scared of him, said Del, a mother sees her child when she wants. And don't call your father by his name.

You do, said Ula.

Beyond the hill was open land, pasture, an old roofless shed split by a tree, a bunched bank of cherrybark oaks, trunks corroded with beetle nests and heart rot. Moss unspooled from the branches. The two of them sat against the split shed. They were hot. It was early June. Del put her hair atop her head and held it there, then let it down. Del was what Clark called "a hard woman," a face like a carving, an eagle-beak nose. She pulled her skirt so high about her waist the hem would not cover her calves. She smelled of ladies' ward—warm milk, disinfectant.

With her own child a mother does what she wants, said Del. She stood and clicked her teeth. She squinted in the sun. I'll show you something I found here, she said, you better not tell at all.

Around the shed were the remains of a mostly picked turnip and cabbage garden. There were tangled rows of weeds and stems. A tomcat lay near dead in the jessamine, panting, mangy orange as an old carpet. Yellow bits of petals flecked its mouth.

Don't you touch it, said Del. Scared me. Damn cat.

He ain't dead, Mama, Ula said. She stepped away.

See there, on his fur those spots like flowers?

Del broke a nail-thin wand off a branch and made a show of poking the tom's tail. She received a small reward—the tom blinked.

Strangest cat I never saw, she said. See that there? You touch his spots, they bloom like t'fire.

No, ma'am, said Ula.

Combustion, you call it, said Del. She pointed to the pearling bulbs of fungus, like a rout of tiny snail shells, on the wand. This, she said, you don't touch this, either.

I wasn't, Ula said.

You touch it—Del rapped the fungus on the wand three times—your hair starts going wild. It's all right for me, see, your mama can touch it.

Del poked the tom again.

But there's another thing around here turns your eyes a color mine is like, she said. That'd be good for you, sure.

Del looked in the grass. Ula knelt amid azaleas and kinked a stem and chewed it.

Her mother felt large, entire, but only half-there, both in this world and out. It's possible, Ula told me, to be motherless while your mother lives. Possible to think of her, even when she's beside you, as a stranger.

See in there? Del pointed to a snake hole. Birds go in there.

No, ma'am.

Oh yes they do. My eyes've seen so. They go in and root. For twigs and seeds.

Del put her head at Ula's level.

You hungry? she said.

We going back? said Ula.

Up here a ways is a place.

From the garden, they found a dirt lane with dwarf magnolia and tiny songs from warblers in the branches. They came to a chipped building, a general store, dull white, the size of a caboose. Strands of Spanish moss hung from the chimney, spiraling down the wide-hipped roof to the eaves. On the porch, a man smoked.

Got anything for me? he said. I ache in this heat.

Sorry, Pop, said Del.

Whose girl is that? he said. That's a pretty dress.

My child. This is mine. Del tapped Ula's head twice.

Is that right? He picked at his shoe. Not likely, he said, she prettier than you.

I'm hungry, Ula said. She chewed the stem and spit the bits into the dirt.

Your father's coming here, said Del.

No, ma'am.

He's meeting us this way. He said so.

In the store was a glass counter with jacks, dice, yo-yos, magazines, and cinnamon chewing gum arranged in neat piles with prices hand-printed on brown paper squares. There was a shelf of pots and pans, flour and sugar on a shelf next to that. Games and puzzles, hardware, cosmetics, and used shoes. There was water damage, the color of camellias, in cracks of the walls. Del eyed a four-cent hair comb. A man in a sweaty work shirt came out from the back. He had large thumbs he held in his pockets.

Dolores? he said. Your nurse ain't come with you?

Meet my family, Quint, said Del.

Hospital know you're here?

This is my daughter. Del tapped Ula's head.

Your child?

Look at her. She's got my face. Look at those shoulders, coming from my own. Del took Ula up under the arms and stood her on the glass counter. She's my blood more than anyone.

Quint put his hand to his hip. I see.

Where's Clark? said Ula.

Del picked Ula up from the counter and placed her on one of the hard wooden stools. Quint brought out a long metal tray. Ula was given soda, ice cream, a cold spoon. She remembered that she rarely received gifts, this ice cream and soda being perhaps her first. It was near dark, and Quint was lighting the outdoor lights.

Look at your little legs, said Del. Got any beaus?

No, ma'am, said Ula.

Your face is a little meaner than mine. But you still will have.

Clark says I'll have long legs, Ula said, he told me.

He's right for once. Look at mine. Del lifted her skirt and held her leg far up straight so that the foot was higher than her face. I danced, she said. She strained to hold her leg. She had a bony white ankle and mosquito bites on her calf. She eased her leg to the floor and fixed her skirt. You want yours long? she said.

With her right hand, she seized Ula's knees, one after the other, her fingers hooking into the sides of Ula's kneecaps.

Now your legs will be, said Del, they'll be long. I made it so.

How long? said Ula.

Longer than mine. Longer than anything at all.

Del had a dime. She bought a three-cent doll that Quint had to stand on his toes to bring down from a shelf. Painted like a harlequin, black triangles above the bald doll's eyes, lashless, arms and legs made of fat peppermint stick wrapped in polka-dot crepe paper.

Her name's Rusalka, said Del.

Ellen, Ula said.

If it's Rusalka already, how can it be Ellen?

It ain't a girl, said Quint.

They came back out onto the dirt lane at dusk. They could see all the way to the side of the levee like a canted roof, down to the main road. When the river rose to two feet from the top, Del told Ula, men guarded at night with guns and lanterns to prevent someone from cutting the levee.

Any rabbits there? Ula said.

We rabbits haven't passed a hundred trees yet, said Del. Not fifty.

Who said that about the guards at night? Clark said?

You listen here, said Del, stopping Ula, looking at her. You won't see him for a while. Not a long while. Now don't you cry about it.

They walked until Ula's legs would not. She'd fallen twice, and there were twigs sticking up from her shoes. She'd never walked so far before—miles—and she felt a deep pain in her ankles like something biting.

I can't walk, she said.

Don't quit now.

The pain spread from ankles to calves and knees. She stopped, put her doll down, and sat in the lane to rub her legs.

You quit that, said Del. You pick Rusalka up and leave your legs alone.

They hurt.

Could be they do, but rabbits don't quit walking. Rabbits never stop.

Something's up inside them moving, Ula said.

Ula stood with her doll and felt the pain in her thighs. Her mother's eyes in the near dark: cold. Pain in her legs burned like cords that would rip. She was crying as they came to a house with a mounted flag, parlor chairs and sofas heaped on the porch. Graffiti was on the door. Empty milk bottles, wires, and broken fencing in small piles in the yard, deep with weeds.

Inside was a grandfather clock and couches tented with sheets. There were rooms with more parlor furniture and mosquitoes and quilts. Del found an old rug and made Ula lie down, and covered them both with the rug.

I can sing to you, said Del. Did you know your mother could sing?

I'm hungry, said Ula.

Del took the doll from under Ula's arm and tore the painted crepe paper off her legs. She broke off each fat peppermint stick leg, gave the right to Ula, and sucked the left herself. It was soft from the heat. Ula asked if anyone was in the house.

They gone, said Del. They been gone.

She lay with her strange hair beside her and told Ula to put her head on it like on a pillow. Everything went dark to the sound of Del sucking the peppermint stick steady as a clock. The orange tomcat who'd eaten jessamine was in Ula's dream. It spit and cackled, a feral orange language Ula didn't know. It wanted something from her, also to tell her something it couldn't—she hated it. When she woke, there was her father and, behind him, the nurse from the ladies' ward. Del had gone.

Clark had Ula's shoulders in his hands.

She was being shaken. Though she'd woken, she was half-not-there. Sometimes you don't come awake for a long time.

FOR STRANGERS

I'm Richard, he said, but I wouldn't remember that later. I'd seen his face before, I told him.

"Is that right? Where was that, sweetheart?"

I'd seen his face on a man in Las Vegas dealing cards, I said, but I've been known to imagine faces from elsewhere in the wrong places, just as I've been known to remember myself in cities I hadn't been. But Vegas had existed—I'd been there. And then Reno, where I lived now. I said something about how in Reno I'd been as directionless as an eastward-walking beetle you pick up off the ground and then turn around to the west and set going again.

"We're *drunk*," he said, putting down his wineglass. He smiled casually, with no sign or glint of keenness inside him.

It was a hotel bar. Amber and white spirits were poured behind me, the bar lit up in a neon blue, with standing clusters of mostly men. A life-sized, plaster Dionysus was in the corner, the hotel was called something-Olympus or Thebes. I was in Sonoma County for a high school friend's wedding, which made Richard and me meeting like this a cliché, and that was erotic, he told me. He was in his early fifties, I supposed, and I was thirty-four. His hair was black, shaggy. He had a pliant nose.

"Are you in the industry?" he said.

"Industry?"

"Wine." He saluted me with his wineglass, a ring with a shallow aquamarine stone on his pinky. He wore two leather bracelets and another of white string. "I am, and this smells like cat piss. Want to smell it? No, you don't. Trust me. You like cats? I've got two. Tabbies. Great, I've known you two minutes and I'm talking about my cats. What a creep." He looked around. "Creep in a bar."

"It's like the inside of a whale," I said. "I'm Jonah."

"Nice to meet you, Jonah." He shook my hand, an exaggerated shake. Veins at his temples showed through the skin.

"Do you know what I want?" I said.

"What?"

"To scare you," I said. "Because I want to."

"What'd you say?" he said.

"Forget it. My name's Paulina, not Jonah."

"You like your name?"

"It's not something to like."

He looked at me with a child's expression of little or no experience. But I liked to think he was smarter than that. I wanted to leave but not yet.

"Paulina," he said. "Pauleeeeena. Can I call you Lena?"

"Why?"

"Because I want to."

Of course not, I said. What about tomorrow? he said. Not ever, I said.

I told him about the rehearsal dinner earlier at the winery. I drank cat piss and ate shrimp and pepperjack cheese cubes on a little plate. The grounds, the tents, the wine were gilded in California's mid-north sun-and-green. My friend the bride was in a white cocktail dress and pink heels; she'd told me on the phone that she had been taking prenatal vitamins to grow her hair long for the wedding. She looked almost the same as seven years before, the last time I'd seen her. All my friendship feelings for her returned, until I remembered we were there for her wedding. She was under strict contract to join the universe of pairs.

"Fucking weddings," Richard interrupted. "Fuck them and their cat piss champagne."

I had been at a table of people I didn't know, though there were a few I recognized from school. I was an isolated friend of the bride's without realizing. People were making speeches while we ate our salads. They were performing their joy, crying. I told Richard I felt the inevitable loping enthusiasm that rises in you from such speeches. I sat next to a guy with long, hare-like teeth in the front. Within five minutes, he told me he was a poet. Oh no, I thought. Oh Lord.

"Oh wow," I'd said.

"Really, I'm a psychiatrist who writes poetry," the guy had told me. "I have a little book. I mostly write for myself."

"I know one poem by heart," I now said to Richard in the bar called something-Olympus-something. "It's called 'A Poem for Strangers.'"

"Oh yeah?" said Richard.

"'A Poem for Strangers,'" I said. "I don't know who wrote it."

"Let's hear it," he said.

"'Hello.'" I paused. I looked up. "That's the poem."

"Say it again," he said. "The whole thing. One more time." He closed his eyes.

"'A Poem for Strangers.' 'Hello.'"

"Oh," he said, opening his eyes. "Hello."

I told him how I'd driven from the winery back to my hotel in Santa Rosa in the dark, into and out of the streetlighting, strip malls, Yum-Yum Burger, Goody Yogurt. Cartoonish names, American fast food. I'd had too much wine. Cat piss, I mean. At first I drove in the wrong direction, to the wrong hotel. A grubby place. I parked in the lot anyway, watching a couple next to a van unload their two children, a gray dog with spots, some luggage, and coolers. A family trip, maybe. The wife's hair tied up on top of her head as she lifted and set down their objects. She looked stressed and busied yet pleased with it all. Some people are chosen to live that way.

"What does that mean?" said Richard. "Some people are chosen—"

"I don't know what I mean. They get to live like that."

"You're saying you want that. Living that way. That's it?"

"You pretend to know lots of shit," I said. "No one wants anything. Nobody. I don't."

"Sure."

"Just coolers," I said. "A van. With spots."

"Is that right?" he said. "Hey, you. Hey. Do you want to see my kid? Isn't that funny, I have a kid?"

"Not really," I said.

He took out his phone and swiped through photos of a miniature girl. She was beautiful.

"That's Roxanne at her birthday party in LA," he said. "We used to live in LA. I used to manage bands. Rock bands. Isn't that funny? I don't normally tell people that. I feel like I can tell you," he said. "Rock bands. My god, did I just say that?"

He put his hand next to mine on the bar, watched for my reaction.

"You haven't asked me anything about myself," I said.

"What?"

"I could be really interesting. You'd have no idea."

"Tell me," he said, putting his phone away. "I'm sorry I haven't. I really want to know."

"I don't want to now," I said.

"No," he said, tapping my hand with his finger. "Hey, you. Hi. Please."

"We can just go."

"Can go?" he said.

"We can go where it is you want."

My hotel room was in a separate building. Large and modern and dark. Inside, a young woman lay crumpled, asleep at the bottom of the stairs, her head beneath her arm, like a bird's beneath its wing. I almost stepped over her but worried about her dignity as I might worry about mine. A corsage—she looked young enough for a prom—was pinned to her dress.

I put my hands on her shoulders, shook her. "Please, love. Please wake up. It's late."

"It's ten-thirty," said Richard.

"Get up," I said to her. "One, two, three."

Without opening her eyes, the sleeping woman woke. "My arm's sleepy. It's asleep. It's sleeeeeeep." She rose up from under her arm and laid her head back on the bottom stair. She tore her corsage with its safety pin from her dress and gripped it and seemed to sleep again. I tried to take the open pin from her hand.

"Give it to me, love," I said to her. "Don't hurt yourself."

She let me take the corsage and close the safety pin. I returned it all to her and closed her fingers back over the battered petals. Then Richard and I went up the stairs. I pushed the key card into its slot, walked in, let him in. He looked at me and put his hand on my cheek.

"What am I doing?" he said. He was acting out disappointment in himself.

"You can leave if you want," I said.

But I wanted him there. We took off our shoes. There was the sweaty, earthy smell of someone's feet, maybe mine. He brought me to the white bed big as a boat and rubbed my back. I'd spent a lot of money on the room, money I didn't quite have, but I felt justified, a reward for having no one to share it with. There was a whirlpool tub, but I wouldn't tell him that.

"I'm married." He stopped, sat up on the bed. "I have a wife. We're very attached."

"You and everybody," I said. "Fine."

"Okay?" he said, rubbing his nose. He lay down again, rubbing my thigh. "Hi, you."

We were kissing, lying the wrong way on the bed. I wondered about his wife without feeling sorry for her. He'd probably called her to say good night when he'd gone to the bathroom at the bar, and she'd felt assured and had gone to bed. I looked to see if he'd taken off his socks and his bare feet were on my pillow, his feet where my head would be later, my hair.

"We should stop," I said. "We should really stop. I need to go to bed."

"But I can rub you like this," he said. "Just until you fall asleep. I'll help you fall asleep."

I took off my dress for him to rub my back, and it felt good for a few minutes. But the room and his hands were so cold.

"I have to go to bed," I said. I turned my head to him but stayed lying on my stomach.

"Two more minutes." He closed his eyes. Then opened them. He was saving this. Saving some image of my face or thighs. Remembering it for later.

I didn't want him, didn't want this. And tried to think forward to the next day at the wedding. Tried to think about my friend. I tried to bring back the image of the family at the grubby hotel. I saw parts of them. Spots on the dog, the mother's hair on top of her head. Her picking up the coolers and putting them on the ground. I wanted to remember everything about her.

"But you can't," I said aloud.

"What?" said Richard.

"You won't remember her."

"Who? Who, you?" said Richard. "Of course I will," he said, drily kissing my back.

"I really have to go to bed," I said.

"Two minutes," he said.

"I'm tired," I said. "I'm serious."

"God. You're so fucking beautiful."

"I'm so fucking tired."

I got up and shook my arms out, a gesture I can't explain. As if I had wings that had gotten wet. I went to the door, standing in only my pantyhose.

"Okay," he said. "Okay, I get it."

He put on his shoes and balled his socks in his pocket and walked out without looking at me. I closed the door right after him and turned up the heat on the thermostat. I picked my purse up off the floor and found a rubber band and put my hair in a high bun.

I was brushing my teeth when I heard someone jiggle the doorknob.

"What are you doing?" I said through the door.

"That woman on the stairs is still there," Richard whispered. "I wanted to come tell you."

"So? Let her sleep."

"And I forgot to tell you a bedtime story," he said. He jiggled the knob. "You need a story."

"I have to go to bed. Stop doing that."

"You need one." He sounded about to pretend to cry and jiggled the knob rhythmically. "You can't sleep without it."

I heard his body slide down the door to the floor. He sat there. I went to the bathroom to rinse out my mouth and toothbrush. He was there when I came back. I could hear him breathing or mumbling.

"Hello?" I called to him through the door. "Are you asleep?"

"I don't know," he said. "It's bizarre out here."

I needed him to leave. And I thought: I was the girl asleep at the foot of the stairs. With the corsage. I'd sleep all night and all day tomorrow, with no strange man at my door. I'd sleep as she slept.

"I'm so tired," he said. "There's no one else in the hallway."

"I know."

"There's nobody. I'm it."

"Some people live that way," I said. "Just live like that, no one there. They're meant to."

"I already," he said, "know that."

SANTA LUCIA

Edward drives Nola to the west edge of town, skidding, almost purposefully, down unplowed, unlit roads. He turns onto the main street—lit hotels, coffeehouses, a bookstore selling two of his books. For driving in winter, he wears a badger fur hat that matches his beard, and he's petting her ear, so small it's nearly nothing.

There's a public garden, dense with roses in spring and summer, then a foreclosed house with a cast stone fountain; they've passed the house many times; this is when Nola invents something for him.

She says, "You know who lived there."

He says, "No."

"The town witch."

"Is that right."

"Oh, yeah. She grew trees with poison berries. All the birds died. She made pies and gave them to her neighbors."

"She didn't bring me any pies," he says.

"That's because this was too long ago," Nola says. "Before you were born. She would have liked you, though, I think."

He's thirty-two years older than Nola. He met her last spring in his undergraduate seminar on the Victorian novel, though he hates the cliché of the professor-student romance. But we're past that, she always says. She graduated in May.

"Are you coming over?" he says.

"I want to."

He lives in a house he bought with his first wife, when he smoked in his study and ashed on his lectures, lectures he cared for, boxes of them, hadn't he? He has a daughter, just here at Thanksgiving, studying law in California, the daughter of his second wife, Christina—Christina, who moved elsewhere.

On his desk are the stacked Russian hardbacks. A photograph of his mother. Eyes flecked with Spain. Postcards from Christina. In the kitchen, Ivan the White barks to be let into the yard full of frosted pyracantha stems and thorns.

"He needs to quit," Edward says when they're in the house. "I'm not chasing him again."

"You're both very bad," Nola says.

They've gone up the stairs. The housekeeper made his bed. The room, with its corner lamps and heirloom armoire, has a carpet stained by the dog. Now it's snowing harder, the window an off-white screen. They've established an order to this. A short while for him to get hard, a short while to come. Afterward he makes a little joke, one line, meaningless, to indicate they've shifted from whatever world of primate ritual into another of comfortable, unextraordinary, postcoital lightness. He half sleeps for ten minutes. By the time he takes her home, his breath is an old man's.

She cracks her knuckles in what he thinks of as carvings of sound, delicate, swift, a pianist preparing to practice, and he tells her so.

"I ordered too much food," he says now. "You'll take some with you."

"We'll see," she says.

In an act of mild perversion, he's invited her to lunch at the faculty club, knowing it becomes, this time of day, a haunt of his department. It's an old-fashioned banquet room with gloved waiters carrying trays of pastry and silver teapots in priestly silence.

"I can't force myself to do things I'm not good at, like play piano," she says. "That's what you're supposed to say is the trouble with my generation, right?"

Her youth, her trump, but he wonders about precocity, how many years it has, if in order to act older, one must be young.

"We'll eat the crabs," he says. "And you take home the lamb."

The department's fellows and one new hire, insular as a Greek chorus, sit at a nearby round table and glance over intermittently. Nola holds her palm above the table's candle. Sleet mud streaks the ankles of her stockings. A short solemn skirt. A paisley barrette. In certain moments, he's convinced she needs gifts. Last year, he bought her a computer, a set of dishes, many books—because he is, almost certainly, taking something from her, a few of her twenty-two years, along with her unironic inquisitiveness, for which he implicitly asks, and reverence. Reverence he feels he returns. He tells himself he most admires her strangeness, which he feels is not invented.

"I had this colleague, he's dead now," he says. "He was in political science. He hated this place, but he always ordered crab and lamb."

"I thought it was a weird combination."

"I think of it as a memorial."

143

She'll eat the lamb as soon as she's home. Will she play with her cat, who "doesn't like men"? She's a year younger than his daughter, similar in a few ways—these facts upset him.

"Why would your friend who died like me?" she says.

"He had exceptional taste; it's why we were friends."

She says, "You only talk about dead people."

"I don't like to gossip."

Remnants of snow dissolve in the carpet. Some flakes melt at the ends of Nola's hair, black, from her Italian father. Wind has chilled her ears and mouth into what Edward calls "frozen treats." She's cracking her knuckles again, quick hands, nothing like his second wife's.

"Tell me about your witch," he says. "I like stories while I eat."

"But we aren't driving."

"Pretend. I suppose she's lovely?"

"Edward." It's Charlie, his department chair, elected to that rank by a strong majority. His little suit is brown, old-fashioned. "Hello, Nola." He gives a small bow. "Edward, I thought you hated the food here." He says this quietly.

"It's the only kind I can eat," says Edward. "I need bland, my doctor says. No spice, no salt."

"Can we have a talk sometime?" says Charlie. "This afternoon, maybe. It isn't about yesterday."

"Which was embarrassing for everyone. We've got to have a real agenda at meetings." This comes out sterner than Edward means, but he likes it and makes his hand into a fist on the table. "Some of us were just sitting there wondering what was happening."

Charlie looks at the new hire and fellows, sitting with some composure as two waiters serve many plates of food.

"I agree," says Charlie. "And I'm working on it. Anyway, there's something else we need to discuss. Can you come to my office? Or maybe we'll talk at the Lucy party. You're coming, aren't you? It's set to snow four more inches tonight, but don't let that keep you away."

"I'll see you tonight."

"Fine, we'll talk then. Bye, Nola." Charlie walks to the fellows' table, and all of them lay down their forks to greet him.

"What's a Lucy party?" says Nola.

"Nothing important," says Edward.

"I thought it was a Christmas party we were going to. What's he going to talk to you about?"

"Charlie's a fucking prince."

"Who's he fucking?" And it comes out wrong, the last word awkward. She folds her hands on the table.

She doesn't take the bus home—he drives her to the bookstore, promising to pick her up at her apartment for the party later. Crab and lamb swing in a bag in her hand as she wipes her boots on a mat. Charlie's son, Andrew, usually away at a small, isolated New England college similar to this one, stands at the front of the store with a red winter nose and a graphic novel.

"That's weird," she says, as the door shuts behind her. "I just saw your father."

"Not weird," Andrew says. "He lives here."

He lacks his father's demonstrative eyebrows. She's met him several times, most recently two years ago at a fraternity party when he introduced himself as Craig and his friend as Schindler.

"Nola, is it right?" he says.

"Mm-hm."

"You look older than last time I saw you."

145

"Colder?" she says.

"Why not? You were graduating. So was my sister. I sat next to your parents."

"I know, they told me," she says.

"I remember because I gave my sister a flower necklace to wear—a real flower necklace that I made of wildflowers I'd picked on the way to the auditorium, you know, a nice gift, I thought—and it was so hot the flowers melted down the front of her dress. She wore white because she reads stacks of wedding magazines, and so her dress was stained orange. It sounds rather pretty, but she didn't think so. She thought it was one of my jokes."

His frugal smile contrasts with his long story, and he's looking at the buttons of her coat while the windows rattle from the wind. He's still holding his book open.

"What book is that?" she says.

"Just rubbish," says Andrew.

"I like graphic novels," Nola says. "Only if they're well done."

"That's easy. I like almost anything well done. Your friend agrees. Ask him."

It's an invitation, or even a faint request, to know more about her understanding with Edward, as if she might answer, We don't talk about books, we only screw. Everyone asks about Edward.

"Are you going to your father's party?" she says.

"His Lucy party?" Andrew says it slowly, rubbing his weak beard. "I could show up. I don't know. I've been around those people most of my life. To be blunt, I think my father doesn't want you there."

"That's not what I was told."

"Suit yourself. I might be going to a house party on Hoffman."

"House parties in this town are rubbish," she says.

"Yes, well, we should meet up. I'm friends with lots of faculty's kids, you know. We've got a merry gang. They'd probably like you. Anyway, we all come in for winter break, only I'm back early. Nobody knows that yet."

He's been tapping the toe of his boot against the bookshelf, making scuffs at the bottom of the blond wood. He's shorter than Edward and more animated, in small ways. She likes this. Likes it quite a bit.

"By the way, don't tell my father you saw me here," he says.

"In town?"

"Of course he knows I'm in town. I live with him. Just don't tell him I was at the bookstore. I'm not ever supposed to be here."

"What? Why can't you be at the bookstore?" says Nola.

"Long story," he says.

Charlie's house—cold floors, dark shellac, art deco mirrors. A square table in the hall with a bowl of Brazil nuts, bottles of rum and wine.

"Why not?" Roman's unzipping his jacket, taking off his hat. His hair is thick and white. "I'm going to bring it up next Tuesday. I mean, no one's stopping you know who from teaching a whole course on—"

"You know her name," says Eric. He's a short man in saggy pants and a shirt.

"If *Amy* insists on teaching a whole course on—" says Roman.

"You mean 'Sex and—"

147

"—Television,' then why not?"

Nola's at the dining room table—spiced apples, apple candles, turkey, glazed ham, stuffing with apricots, miniature truffles, Scottish tea.

With a full plate, she leaves the dining room. In Charlie's living room, a large, red-faced man with tartan socks holds a plate of turkey and ham on his lap. One of two women in wobbly, doll-like chairs turns to Nola.

"You came with Edward, right?"

"Yes," says Nola.

"Charlie invited you? I'm Molly, Eric's wife. This is Katherine."

"It's so cold in here," Katherine says, hunching, pushing her skirt down over her knees. There are dark red veins in her eyes.

"And I've got some kind of cramp. Excuse me, but I do," says Molly. She overpronounces her words.

"Christ, how weird," says Katherine. "I have a cramp, too. I wonder if our cycles are aligned."

"I don't know but I'm ready for the Lucy rolls."

"What's Lucy?" Nola says.

Molly looks as if she might say something else but then finishes her eggnog and places the glass between her knees. She buttons the top button of her sweater.

"Saint Lucy. Nola, sit down," Molly says. "We're curious about Edward—he's very unpredictable, we think."

Again, the questions about Edward. From the corner, a seventy-five-year-old Chaucer scholar Nola didn't notice clears her throat in two ascending notes, the second with a slightly whimsical adornment, while holding her mouth in a curious bassoonist's embouchure. Saint-Saëns's "The Dying Swan" plays on the stereo.

"I drink tea," the Chaucerian says. "It's full of antioxidants. I'd love tea if I didn't drink it every day," she continues. "But I drink it every day because I like it so much." Her mouth gives way to slight spasms at its corners. The red-faced man in tartan socks nods politely.

"That's very true, Diana," Katherine says loudly, with unintended condescension, as if speaking to a great-aunt from whom one stands to inherit a small house or large jewel. "Tea is a great pleasure for us all."

"The paintings are awful." Molly gives a hissing sound. She squeezes the tassels of her scarf, then wraps the whole scarf around her neck in three turns. "But I'm not going to say that to Charlie. It would hurt him. I wonder if he has some kind of muscle relaxer. I really do have a cramp."

Nola walks by a side table with a photo of Andrew in profile, his nose pointed toward a huddle of wary new fellows and their husbands in a corner. She enters the screened-off patio.

"Hello." Roman's smoking in a wicker chair. He's wearing a black T-shirt. He's stuck his long legs out so that Nola must walk over his feet to the other side of the patio. "Are you eating? What good things Charlie has. I like turkey very much. Do you?"

"I do," she says.

"Oh, you do?" He's encouraged. "You like turkey?"

"Yes, with stuffing."

"I like stuffing. All that with rum. Christmas rum sent down from Jesus. Cookies, you like those?"

"You sound like Edward," she says.

"What about . . . bread and butter?" Roman sits up in his chair.

He's obnoxious, she thinks. Would she ever have been charmed by him?

"Bread with butter?" she says.

"It's simple, I know, but it's overlooked. I try not to overlook anything."

Edward's at the doorway. "I didn't know you were out here. Aren't you cold?"

"We were just talking about our favorite foods," Roman says.

"Foods?" Edward comes to Nola and says the word softly, drowsily.

"Nola seems to like all foods equally," Roman says.

"I didn't say that," says Nola.

"No? I thought you did."

"This is an odd misunderstanding," Edward says.

"There's no such thing as an odd misunderstanding," Roman says. "No such thing as a normal one."

"Roman—"

"We were having a conversation, Edward, and I don't even like conversation."

"Doing all right?" Edward talks directly into Nola's ear. He thinks he needs to look after her, but he knows so little of what she needs now. Once, she thought he knew.

"Edward." Charlie's at the porch door. He's in the same brown suit as before. "Hello, Nola. Roman. Edward, I need to speak with you"—working his jowls—"let's come inside."

"Not tonight," Edward says. "I'm feeling a little funny now."

"I don't mind leaving early," Nola says.

"Charlie, that meeting the other day. It was . . . ," Roman says, "not to be repeated, as far as I'm concerned."

"Well I've spoken with Edward about it, haven't I?" Charlie says. "Spoken with a few others. We'll figure it out. Edward, let's come inside and talk."

"Charlie, what is this?" Eric shouts from the house.

"That isn't the point," Roman says.

"Charlie?" Eric shouts. "Where'd you get *this*?"

"Let's go in." Edward takes Nola's elbow. "You coming?"

"All right," she says. "Let's go soon, okay? Leave the party, I mean."

"Of course," says Edward.

Roman rises from the wicker chair. "I'll go with you."

Roman, Edward, and Nola walk into the house to hear Eric shouting: "Hey, Charlie! Come in here a second!"

Eric's in the dining room, a plate of food in his hand. He's in front of a shelf the length of the wall, examining an antique pistol in a faux velvet cushioned case with a glass hatch.

"It's a funny thing for you to have," says Eric. He inserts an entire dreidel-shaped cookie into his mouth and chews it while readying his right hand with another from his plate.

"It came from my grandfather's farm in Pennsylvania," says Charlie, extracting the pistol from its transparent coffin. "I asked for it when he died." Edward takes the gun in his one drinkless hand and grasps the barrel. Nola grabs Edward's shoulder.

"I've heard about these Pennsylvania farms," says Roman. "I knew a man who had one, in fact. On a Pennsylvania farm, you've got to have a certain number of animals to have the privilege of calling it a farm. You've got to have that amount. No matter what. So this man I knew lived in New York. He hired a couple of guys to look after his Pennsylvania farm. A couple of rascals. I met these guys in Pennsylvania.

151

"I spent a weekend there," says Roman. "Anyway, there weren't enough animals on the farm. Now the man with the property—this was a smart man, a lawyer in New York— needed a *farm* for tax purposes. So how do you think he did it? How did he have enough animals?"

"What does this have to do with anything?" says Nola.

Katherine comes into the room, leading the Chaucerian, shuffling clumsily, toward the bathroom.

"Goodness, a gun," says Diana. Her long skirt is stained with cranberry. "No, I don't feel well at all. Not one minute of it or any of them."

"Please, it would be a good idea to calm down," says Katherine. She's dabbing at Diana's skirt with a red, crumpled napkin as they walk. Katherine's eyes are hazy, without focus.

"Can I help?" says Nola.

"We're okay," says Katherine. She shuts the bathroom door.

"He brought in goats?" says Edward, turning to Roman. "Lots of goats?"

"Not goats," Roman says. "How else do you think the lawyer did it? For the farm?"

"Hired more rascals," says Eric.

"No," Roman says. "Rabbits." His eyes become larger. "Rabbits."

Edward stares at the stripes on Roman's sleeve. "Where the hell did you get that shirt?"

"What do you mean?" says Roman. "This is my boring shirt."

"Before I forget," says Charlie, coming between them. "Time for these." He uncovers a tray of saffron rolls beneath their noses. "Lussekatt, Lucy buns. I made these. We're a week early now for Saint Lucy's Day, but that doesn't matter."

152

"It occurs to me," says Roman, with a slow lilt. "Every year we have little Lucy rolls, but aren't we supposed to have a procession? With a Lucy to lead us? Charlie, you're half-Swedish, isn't that what's done?"

"Yes, there's a Lucy," Charlie says. "She wears a crown with candles."

"Well it's our first Lucy party," says Roman, "where I believe we have a Lucy, gentlemen."

Nola knows he is looking at her but refuses to look back. She wouldn't mind being Lucy, but she minds Roman.

"That isn't a good idea." Charlie pulls apart an S-shaped roll and squeezes it nervously into his mouth.

"Roman," says Edward very loudly, sloshing a bit of the nog from his cup. "That's not the point. I'm talking about your shirt. It's making me damn dizzy."

"You ought to be grateful," Roman says. "We have Lucy."

"As long as nobody sings," says Edward. "I don't want anyone to sing."

"You're our Lucy," Roman says to Nola.

"I got that," she says.

"You know Lucy," Roman says. "Lucy our saint. All right, now what you're going to do is walk around in a circle while we sing. Eric was a chorus boy, an asthmatic chorus boy, but nevertheless. So, Nola, walk all around. There you are. We don't have any candles. Charlie, start singing?"

"I don't want Charlie to sing," says Edward.

"No thank you, Roman," says Charlie. "I won't sing."

"But what are the *words*?" says Roman.

"I remember," says Eric.

Edward bites a saffron roll while Eric sings "Santa Lucia" in his countertenor. Roman takes out a lighter and flicks the flame and hands the lighter to Nola. She walks the perimeter of the room, holding the flame just below her chin, laughing a little. Charlie looks impatient.

"Edward," says Charlie.

"Roman, you sing, too," Eric says.

"No thanks," Roman says. "Quite winded."

"All of us," Edward says. "*Sit down!*"

"Edward, please." Charlie takes Edward's arm. "Edward, come now. Time for our talk."

They go, coatless, through the porch door, under bare branches, into the snow, not vanishing as it hits the ground. Edward no longer feels drunk; this is something else. In the house what sounds like a wineglass breaks.

"What was that?" Charlie says.

"Snowflakes," says Edward. "They're strobing. Water's coming off at different angles."

"Jesus, how much have you had?" Charlie looks at Edward's glass. "Listen, I've been wanting us to talk. You can probably guess what it is." Charlie walks ahead to a shrub covered in long flanks of snow and stops, and Edward sways as he walks. No, this isn't drunkenness. He doesn't know what this is.

"No, Charlie," says Edward. "It is I who must speak with *you*."

"Oh?"

"Charles, what's this?" He points to Charlie's head.

"What's what?" says Charlie.

"It isn't even you. It isn't even yours."

"What's wrong with you?"

"Right there. I guess I have to try to pull it off." Edward throws his glass in the snow. With spread hands, he grabs Charlie's head, as if to heal a sinner at an evangelical revival.

"Edward, really, what the hell?"

Edward lurches back. Charlie is talking; Edward doesn't understand. Edward sprints to the house.

"They're spotted. It's just bad art." At the center of a small crowd, Molly makes large, vague swipes at her right hand with her left. Her sweater is on the floor. Both straps of her dress have fallen from her shoulders. "Eric, let's go. Let's go. Let's go. Let's go."

"Molly! Molly, quit." Eric whispers in her ear. "Please just put your cup down."

"Little bits of cinnamon, I swear," she says. "I tried to lick them off at first, didn't I, Katherine? Katherine? Where is she? Where'd she go?" She begins to weep. "What ages me?"

"Eric, do you feel all right?" Charlie says.

"I'm fine," Eric says.

"Who the Jesus put so many mirrors in this house?" says Roman. "Fifty, forty-nine, forty-eight, forty-seven . . . It's like an orgy in here, so many redundant bodies, no sex. But never the sex. Never the sex? Christ, something's finally wrong with me."

"Roman, please. What in God's name is happening here?" says Charlie. "What's wrong with Edward?"

"Strange cock," says Edward. "Very strange cock. I swear it isn't even yours. Right there on your head, Charles."

Everyone looks at Charlie, except the fellows and the new hire, and their three husbands, the six of them standing together, largely mute, until one of the husbands, a young, stooped man, who after looking around the room as if for a bit of confidence, raises his right arm triumphantly and shouts, "My ribs are swollen!"

"I know what I smell—it's opopanax!" says Edward. He attempts to unzip Nola's purse, hanging from her shoulder.

"Someone's put LSD in the eggnog," says the husband with swollen ribs.

Edward looks at Nola's hands. Thousands of freckles, freckles on top of freckles.

"Edward?" says Nola. "You had the eggnog? I didn't have any."

"Christ, he's right," says Roman. "It's fucking LSD. I said this eggnog tasted shit-like."

"Calm down, please." Charlie's holding Edward by the wrist. "Nobody's spiked your eggnog."

"LSD! It's LSD. I'm a fucking kid again," Roman says in the middle of the living room. "Look at all these jerks with cups of nog."

Molly sits on the sofa, crying with both hands over her mouth.

"You're insane," says Charlie. "You think there's LSD?"

The bathroom door slams open—Katherine says, "I'm taking Diana to the hospital. Someone needs to come help me with her. Eric. Do you hear me? Diana's in the bathroom. Eric."

"Jesus Christ," says Charlie, watching Molly try to stand up. "My kid. Jesus Christ. Andrew. He thinks I won't have him arrested."

The Saint-Saëns recording restarts, and the man in the tartan socks comes into the room with a new plate of turkey and says, "My first wife used to love this piece."

* * *

Nola's never driven his car before tonight. Edward takes his badger hat from the glove box and reclines his passenger seat. The roads are full of coarse tracks of snow.

She knows how he thinks of her, and this is what she takes from him—his myth of her, his subtle romanticization. But she's through with that. On her first paper he'd written, "Adept." She thinks that word now. No, she unthinks it. That word is too good for him.

"Your hair is my wires." Edward puts on his hat.

"Close your eyes," she says. "Lie back down."

"Your eyes are witch way hazel. Your witch with berries."

"But I'm not the witch," she says. "Not at all."

"I want to tell you what I'm seeing right now."

"Tell me."

LITTLE MOON

The three men faced her, seated shoulder to shoulder along a plank against the vibrating steel wall. They called the girl's small brother Mine.

Mine, that's mine, the boy had said to the girl for hours. He slept across their mother's legs, their mother asleep on another plank, her black skirt crumpled in his fist and tugged above her knees. They were leaving their village in a truck with no windows. A camping lantern swung from a hook. The girl thought it was night, or near that, and she wasn't tired.

The truck stopped, no one got up. The amplitude of the lantern's swing increased. A pale wood crutch lay on the knees of a man, and he took from his pocket a long match and lit it on the crutch's rubber tip. On his cheek was a violet-black mole the girl imagined might come alive.

I dislike sleep, he told the girl, matches keep me awake. He blew out the flame. On the toe of his boot, he lit a second match; he brought the flame to his face, then teased the stubble on his chin with the flame. The drivers were outside—"stretching my legs," one of them said. She could hear them

159

unwrapping food and popping cans and talking on phones. The drivers were paid, said the man with the crutch and the flame near his face, a considerable price. Those men are costly.

The truck's hold, a small, dim cube, had a wall of boxed microwaves between the passengers and the loading port. The girl imagined being pulled by horses over pitted roads. One white with spots. It liked to eat apples at stops. Closing her eyes, passing through the screen of her inner lids, she entered Somewhere Else, where a horse eats roses from a dusty bush. Inside a rose, a line of ants circles around the same path. The rose is thirsty.

She woke to the lantern swinging on its hook. The man with the crutch on his knees was whistling, only breath, no resonance. She decided it was very late; the other two men on the plank were asleep. She decided they were cousins, or brothers. She decided there was such a thing as brother-cousins. They had on jeans and long-sleeved shirts, one man's shirt was ripped at the armpit. The matchman was the oldest. Eyelids thin as folding paper. On the knee of his jeans, he struck two flames at once and whistled.

I'm damn tired, he said. I've got meanness in my dreams.

He blew out the match and lit another and whistled again, through the gap where a tooth was not. Mine woke, and so did their mother; she pushed her skirt down.

You hear that? said the man. Hear it now? He had the match to his ear.

The girl asked her mother how matches made flames.

They're cursed things, her mother said and looked at the man.

Mine had taken off his sneakers and was crawling on the truck floor, the bottoms of his white socks dark from dirt, and every now and then he scratched his heel. Smaller than he should be, everyone told her mother that. In the corner, next to the rip-shirted man's work boot, Mine found a length of wire, faded metal, kinked in one place, and he threw it up and caught it, each time with a surprised laugh.

Give it, said their mother. This minute. She fanned herself with an advertisement she'd folded into an accordion. The lantern shone on the sweat in the V-shaped creases at the corners of her eyes.

Mine threw the wire down the length of the truck. It shimmered as it flew. The man with the crutch reached down with difficulty and took up the wire, and Mine reached the man, and the man dangled the wire over Mine's face.

Mine, said the man.

Mine grabbed for it. The man tick-tocked the wire, click-tocking his tongue.

Mine.

Mine was on his knees, holding up his hands, waiting should the wire drop.

Mine's a kitten, said the girl.

The matchman was awake but seemed to be dreaming. He bent over, paused in the air, saying a few things she could hear, a few she couldn't, the sound of the words, not the sense. He sat up and leaned out to touch a thing not there. Then he woke and yielded and brought his hand back.

Got something, the man said.

He took a clear ball from his pocket and bounced it and caught it. His crutch rocked on his knees.

Do you know what this is?

He bounced the ball, softly enough not to wake anyone, not her mother, not even Mine in her mother's lap.

161

You know what this is? Fortune-teller ball. Tell me what you want.

I don't know, the girl said.

This ball knows. It will tell you. In Los Angeles you will have a lipstick. In Los Angeles you will have a kitten.

He bounced the ball and let it roll to the end of the truck by the microwave boxes and took a match from his pocket. He lit it on his teeth. A vertical wrinkle split his face from forehead to lips, which leaked a little orb of spit. He dashed his finger over the flame.

He said, Look, I'm a clown.

He blew out the match. He repeated his trick—this match took five strikes on his teeth.

Try, he said. He held it to her. No?

I don't know.

Come here. I'll teach you.

He pointed to the little space between himself and the rip-shirted man, still asleep.

Come, he said.

She squeezed herself into that space. The matchman's gut fell over his belt; his breath was bitter oranges. His eyes had no lashes. She was staring.

Fortune abandoned me, he told her.

He took out another match and let her look at it. Very quickly, he flicked it on the denim on her knee. It didn't light.

Stop, she said.

So? You want to try?

She did. I don't know, she said. She didn't.

He flicked another on her skirt.

Tell this match the things you want, he said.

He took a match and put it next to her mouth.

Stop, she said.

He flicked it on her teeth, no flame.

Don't!

He flicked it on his own, it lit. He held it to her face.

See? he said. Very easy.

She decided it was dawn. Only Mine was awake. The match-man's hat brim sloped down over his eyes. The man whose shirt was whole snored and then snorted in his sleep like her horse eating roses. Roses from the dusty bush. Eating ants in the roses from the dusty bush. In the narrow space between the men's boots and the little drawstring bag her mother held between her feet, the children sat, drawing invisible pictures with their fingers on the corrugated floor. Mine's finger, drawing a broad arc, found a match. He held it in the beam of lamplight.

Give it to me, the girl said. She took it from Mine and held it to her mouth. Look, I'm a clown. Look, she said again, with a deep voice. I'm a clown. What's your fortune?

She meant to scare him. Mine cried his name and swiped the match. He held it to his own mouth like a moustache.

Careful now, she said. It'll break.

He opened his mouth, a few tiny teeth, and put the black tip in.

Don't, she said. Don't do it. You'll die.

She took the match away, and he cried his name. She thought their mother would wake.

See? she said. Look. Look at me now.

She flicked the black tip against her top teeth, splitting the match as it flicked, one half flying away.

Dead! Mine said.

As he crawled toward the match, the truck jerked him onto his back, and he stuttered the beginning of a curse word he'd heard their mother say. The truck slowed, stopped, and the drivers' radio was turned off. Their mother and all of the men were awake. The matchman steadied his crutch.

Shut Mine up, said the rip-shirted man. He dropped from the plank to his knees and pressed his hand across Mine's mouth.

Give him here, the mother whispered.

She held him, pressing her hand across his mouth. He twisted and tried to scream. The other brother-cousin turned off the lantern.

For many minutes stopped in the dark the girl stayed on the floor. Nothing would happen, her mother had told her yesterday. Just be quiet if we stop. The girl rubbed her feet together and felt the rubber soles of her shoes. She imagined they were in an upside-down barnacled ship, sunk to the ocean's bottom. She can breathe underwater. In her head, she makes words and drawings—her own name, in cursive, the way she learned it, the loops in the letters becoming malformed animals—she gives six arms to a hippo *M* . . . she puts a tortoise head on a dolphin *P*. The animals swim above her. Her horse with its head in the water and its mouth full of rose lipstick.

The truck finally moved. The matchman turned on the lantern, and their mother let Mine go. He gave a resentful push against her chest and squirmed to the floor. There was a plastic water jug; the two cousin-brothers passed it back and forth while Mine looked for wires and matches. The matchman asked for a drink.

She'd been asleep for hours and woke in the lamplight to the rip-shirted brother grinning and sputtering in his sleep. Maybe he was in a dream. Maybe he was in a TV show dream. A game show. Maybe he was answering questions, winning prizes.

She'd been on the floor a long time, drawing with her finger a zoo of impossible animals in aquariums and cages, shark teeth in the mouths of giraffes. The truck stopped.

Jesus.

What the hell, the drivers yelled, and other muffled things.

The drivers left the truck, slamming doors, leaving the engine and radio on. Her mother had woken and covered Mine's mouth, this time with the child gone limp without complaint. The cousin-brothers had their ears against the metal wall. One put up his arm and shrugged, as if to say he heard nothing.

The girl waited.

The matchman looked as if he might sneeze. It's very bad when adults are scared.

There was a great bang at one end—the truck was being opened, without the signal they'd agreed on with the drivers. Someone turned off the lamp.

Come on out.

You all be quiet, whispered the matchman. Stay and say nothing.

Come on out, said one of the drivers. It's all right, we arrived miles ago. He'd lifted up the door of the truck and was taking apart the wall of microwave boxes.

You're taking this all down? said the second driver. You'll just have to put it back together.

We don't need to put it back, now that we're here.

Daylight through a hole in the wall—the girl shut her eyes. A grainy breeze against her face.

Come out, now, said the driver. You have to see this.

The second driver helped the first with the boxes. More and more daylight, at the very top and then through scattered gaps in the wall. Then a door-shaped hole in the wall. Most of the boxes were open and scattered on the ground now; so many had been empty.

You have to see, said the first driver, holding out his hand to the rip-shirted brother, who looked away. No?

The driver looked at the girl. You want to come see?

She couldn't see his face in the hard sunlight. She took his hand and stepped out, her mother, holding Mine, behind her. They'd parked the truck on the side of the road. There were no other cars. Flies zigzagged in her face. A flock of birds scavenged a gutted suitcase.

You all need to see this, the driver said to the men in the truck. You only see this maybe one time in your life. There's nobody out here, okay? I promise. Nobody.

The men came to the door-shaped hole.

What's going on?

Small steps, old man. No falling.

The drivers led everyone beyond the road, into a plain of dirt. A place without trees or green. Mine tried to free himself from his mother's arms so he could walk. They were going toward a strange, raised ring of dust, a small crater in the earth.

It's a hell of a welcome, said one of the drivers.

Wait till you see it, said the other, wiping his nose with his hand. We saw it come down.

They came closer to the little crater in the dirt. Smoke rose from its rim, where the dirt had rutted and turned rust-colored and black. Pungent smell of underground, of turned-up earth. Earthworms curled in the soil. Inside the crater was a foot-long piece of charred, rocky metal.

166

The drivers and the cousin-brothers surrounded it, and the matchman stood back. The girl's mother let Mine down to the ground, though she held him. He wanted to touch the rocky metal. He shrieked his name. One of the drivers paced around the crater several times, watching the thing inside as though it might move. Grooves and holes in it in a random pattern. A little metal moon.

The matchman sat in the dust a few feet from the moon. He looked as though he wanted to sleep, but he watched the brothers, who took his crutch and poked at the moon with the crutch's tip. A driver came back with gloves on and an oily cloth. He crouched and picked up the metal thing, still smoking, and blew on it.

Goddamn, he said.

The girl went to him. She looked at the moon-thing, scabbed and pitted and smoking, that had fallen so near without her knowing. A few ants moved beside her shoe. Maybe looking for water.

EYE OF WATER

A minute of rain then none of it. The desert again itself. As if
I should thank life for a bit of rain, and I don't.

Desert, Isaac tells me, is what the sea became. Here is what
the desert once was: wet and ivory-green and all we lack. It's
something we talk about before doing other things, like TV,
room service, sex. He sleeps. We're in a hotel on the Strip,
though we both live in apartments a few miles away—we want
to feel we've had a night out in our own town. We're tired of
the bed in my apartment.

I take a picture with my phone of the skyline pinking to
black, Tropicana Avenue, east-west. Inside all this: magicians,
aerialists, waiters, dealers, comedians, acrobats, and women
and men throwing their chips in small caves at green felt tables.

Isaac's snoring. His stomach, warm bear-pudge, rises and
falls; his blue jacket is on the floor. His socks I've taken off,
and plaid boxers, jeans, T-shirt with the name of a band I don't
know. His thin glasses are on the table. He's my age, thirty-one,
though we've said neither of us feels it. I go to the bathroom,
big as the bedroom in my apartment, and wash my face. A

169

luxury. Hotels on the Strip give you water; it's all recycled, but you pay for it. Hotel soaps wrapped in printed paper, big as medallions, are free, but for water you pay.

I'm alive in a desert, having once driven in, not yet come out. Cactus and tufts and mounds of weeds. An expanse long as the notes of warblers in the West, Cash and Presley. I sing, too. Opera once. I traveled anywhere, if they'd have me—Gilda in *Rigoletto* in Milwaukee, Norina in *Don Pasquale* in St. Louis. I moved to Vegas to sing in a club. They need me, I think. I'm that good here. When all the water goes, so will this music that greens my life.

I leave Isaac asleep in the morning, buy coffee at a donut place in the casino, pick up my car from the valet, and drive home. I pay too much for my downtown apartment. There's a cactus in a clay pot by my bed. Clark County doesn't allow plants, except cacti. I say, take water from gamblers, don't starve living things, but I don't run a city. I have two glasses of water a day while sitting in my yard of rock. Not gravel—rock, brown and dun and dim white. I sit in a cushioned chair, stained with the bright urine of a neighbor's dehydrated tabby tom. He is bloated, his fur withered. Part wild, he eats the rodents that forage our Dumpsters.

My ex-husband lives in Venice with a woman named Marisol. Venice. Once when I was drunk I told him I'd go there when the water's gone. The Mojave is the driest desert in North America. Lake Mead is drying up, and the project they'd been hoping would bring more water was abandoned a year ago.

In my bathroom, I drink whiskey and line my eyes Klimt-gold. I draw a star on my forehead. A feather boa around my neck. I'm no pigeon, but a starry peacock. A peahen. A carnivorous, whiskeyed peahen.

I go to work at the club at four. It's late November and dark so soon and cold for our desert. I don't hate the club, I'm used to it, and peahens with whiskey neats in their hands can be Earth's happiest creatures. To the house beat, my hips are alive, devoted. Hip, hip, all of you on the spotlit dance floor, light parading atop your skulls. You forget the city's drying up. In the bathroom—the toilet costs five dollars to flush—you insert tokens purchased from a bartender into a meter installed on the flush lever. Of course, most people don't flush. There have been many overflowing toilets. There's a hundred-dollar fine for that.

I've put an ad in the classifieds for a roommate. The math works out that you have more water with two people. Not very much more, but I have a two-bedroom; the second room I don't use. Tonight I'm meeting someone who called me with a deep voice, as if ash inside, welled up from the chest. Willa. Some life in her voice, the weight of it.

I sing in a lounge behind the club, a square room gilded on all four sides to make drunk VIPs conjure palace ceilings of Versailles, and I the court musician, singing dry, my neck long and taut for thee.

I told Manny to let her in, and there she is at the bar. Willa, with a glass of water. That's ten dollars.

"Some guy bought it for me," she says. "This place is like things used to be."

What I notice first is her jewelry—she wears too much. Several necklaces. Bangles up her wrist and stackable rings. All of it chintzy, flimsy. She immediately puts her hair up in

171

one motion, a glossy dark-blonde twist, fastening it with a clip she unclips from her bra. Her face reminds me of a statue in Rome, from which the hands had fallen. I had voice lessons there one summer. Hers—Willa's—is a perfectly rounded nose. Eyes a bit close together.

"You work here?" says Willa. "Or what? You do what here," she says, blinking twice.

"I sing," I say. I'm a peahen in a gold room with a few regulars who wait for me. Who imagine all kinds of things when they watch me sing, maybe their pert cocks in my mouth.

I do not want to think of Willa as a bird, but do. Think of one that's fallen to the sidewalk, perched, alive but rumpled, not quite what she was before. There's a scarred gash along one side of her neck with a layer of concealer on top.

"I like this," says Willa, holding up her water. "This is *good*. It's real."

Sometimes in bars and casinos they dilute water with gin, a little cheaper, which no one complains about.

"You want some?" she says.

I take the smallest sip and hand back the Communion cup.

I decide I want her with me and tell her so. I lower the rent by seventy-five dollars before she says anything, and she says it's a deal, her voice higher suddenly. I order a whiskey. We clink. She says she'll move in this week.

There's a band onstage, five of us. I'm at the mike in front of Jon on the drums. I'm better than usual, and loud, singing for my new friend Willa in that gold room. I'm the Distractor: no one's thinking about water now, or dry lips. After the first two Irving Berlin numbers, she's gone from her barstool. Goodyman sits in the front row. Biting his cheek. Thumbing his smartphone. Watching me.

"Little girl, that star on your forehead shakes when you sing," he says after the first set. He tips me a roll of toilet flush coins. Goodyman loves Irving Berlin.

There have always been two intake pipes, two straws, they call them, from Lake Mead to Las Vegas, shuttling water. Then the lake water began to leave. To save us, when the water sank below the first straw they made plans to bore a tunnel for a third pipe. Water, dear to us as holy water to a pilgrim.

Indoor water was recycled. The population increased. Water for outdoors was a luxury. Within three months, the county pulled up all the residents' grass. I have never needed green more than when it left me.

Pools were drained. Selling grass seed was illegal. Casinos lobbied to keep grass and water for landscaping, for precious golf courses; they needed it, they said, for the economy. Then Lake Mead, which we took for granted, sank below the second pipe. Plans for the tunnel they'd been hoping to build failed: there were delays and barriers; the project never happened.

It was cost-efficient to decrease the population, we were told. But they couldn't make us leave. The state took over water companies. By law, meters were installed on all residential faucets and showers. On faucets and toilets in public bathrooms, too. We were allowed 7,000 units every two weeks at home. A glass of water was 175 units; a bath, 6,000. Next year, they said. Wait until next year. Next year will be worse.

Isaac and I tried to calculate things. They must ship water in from Lake Powell, charging much more than it cost. They wanted us out. Living in a desert would lay us bare. Half the population left; businesses relocated. So many neighborhoods abandoned; we were a ghost town in a living country. But Vegas has more tourists. The spectacle draws them to us.

Isaac and I have a game called Then What.

"Then what happens? When the water's all gone?" he says.

"They'll ship us out to space," I say. "We'll live on a pod. Just Vegas."

"Then what?"

"I'm leaving you for the first pro poker player I find," I say.

"And then?"

"We'll have a kid we'll name Max Bet."

"No, really," he says.

"I told you," I say. "Venice."

Willa comes two nights later, with an old-fashioned trunk as big as me, several tote bags, a laundry basket full of clothes and hats, a box of books. She takes the first month's rent check out of her bra and hands it to me. Her room has a bed with a stained mattress, sheets, a bookshelf, last year's calendar. The first thing I do is adjust the Faucet Meters in the bathroom and kitchen: our quota's more than what mine alone was.

She goes to the kitchen and makes herself a small glass of water. The red digits on the Faucet Meter go up by one hundred.

"It's okay," she says. She looks at me. "Promise."

We bring the Meters to the Water Center every two weeks. As roommates, we have sixteen thousand units per week. Eight thousand units each. If you have less on your Meter than your allotment, you get cash back. If you go over, there's a fine. Go over three times, they turn off your water for a month. Willa drinks two long swallows. I hear water shuttling down. All those units gone down her throat.

"You look nervous," she says. "Are you a nervous person? It's something I should know, if we're living together."

"Sometimes," I say. "Like everybody."

"Oh, honey," she says, watching me. "That's not like everybody."

We sit on the couch. It's a strange apartment, large and shabby. Comfortable. Tape on cracks in the windows, a worn sofa and a couple of armchairs. I love living this way, economical and a little rustic. I've been here two years.

Willa's dark blonde hair falls straight around her neck over that long gash she covers with makeup. Sun-spotted skin beneath her eyes. There's a green eye tattooed on her wrist—a garnet-sulfur eye under her bracelets. She has on a cropped leather jacket. She is palpably sad and talkative, about a boy she just left. Packed up her things in her station wagon and came here, she says. Her hands reveal her; she doesn't know where they should go.

"He was giving too much," Willa says. "He didn't have a job for a long time. He used to work for the Water Center before it was taken over. He gave so much that I didn't know what he had for himself. Have you felt like that ever?"

"Sure," I say. "At some point, probably."

"I ended up sorry for him." She laces her hands in front of her chest and holds them there for a second, solid, composed. "You know how that happens?"

I don't; it seems unnecessarily complicated.

"We should get you a drink," I say. "A drink drink. To celebrate you coming."

"And some more water?" she says.

"Really? More?"

"Oh, god," she says. "You're a worrier. I could tell."

Of course I'm not. Speaking of water, I say, I'm not bathing every day, and of course I don't think she should.

"Honey, that's gross," she says.

I go to the kitchen and fill her water glass half full and open two beers. She loves to talk. She recites her horoscope. She says she once had a dream about sex with a wolf, and there are more details, but she won't say what. Once she lived in Tonga for three months and worked for her grandfather's company, pollinating vanilla plants. My parents are elementary school teachers, I tell her. And everyone has strange dreams.

Goodyman works for the state, so he says. He's promised me a deal at the Southern Nevada Water Center. Three thousand more units, at least, in lieu of a tip. He's drunk when he offers deals. He'd say anything to get things he wants. I mention this to Willa in the morning, and she makes herself another glass of water. He wants to fuck you, she says. He despises me, too, I say.

I have a work permit that means, should the time come, they won't make me leave. I entertain on the Strip, I'm a commodity. I could sing waterless if I have to. Willa says her father was in the army, that veterans' families get privileges, too. She's moved in with two secret plants, black market ferns, and she waters them every two days. A man sells them in a tent in the lot behind Atomic Liquors.

"I didn't even see you bring these in."

"Look, it's completely fine," she says. "I need things growing. I need green. Otherwise, I just can't. Nothing works. I've got no life without them."

As soon as the words leave her, I feel they are mine. I tell her that this is what I've thought, have always thought. Green.

Her ferns are shining, clean. Greener at their centers than I've seen. Ours now, I want to say.

I bring out my state-approved cactus.

"Susannah," she says. "You little *devil*. Let me show you what else I've got."

She brings a compact rectangular pot of soil, a tiny herb garden. Six herbs, including mint and parsley and tansy, ragged leaves like worn pages cocked down to the soil, near dead from stale air. An occult scent I never knew. Healing and hot.

"The fern man in the tent had it," Willa says.

"They need water," I say. "Lots and lots and lots of water."

"You don't need to tell me," Willa says. "Let's water the hell out of them."

I make a small, high-pitched noise, a squeal I've never heard come from me. This is what I wanted without knowing. And I do it, *I* do it, a whole glass. Slowly at first, then all of it. If the Water Center fines us, we'll drop the cash on the desk and leave. I've seen others do it. I've seen people throw green bills in state employees' faces. Willa takes off her bracelets to run her hands under the water. The green tattooed eye on her wrist winks at me. She bends until her head drops down to the faucet to drink from it. She is wild as any green I might imagine she owns.

"Damn it, bring your ferns, too," I tell her.

"Yes, ma'am." She salutes.

I give them water, and now we're greedy. Bright streams of green unlock. We promise—we write on a piece of paper, we sign: "We will water them every day." I line up our plants on the counter. I make myself a glass of water. Our garden smells of salty, green life. I break off the tip of a mint leaf and eat it.

This is the way you see *into*: Eye of water. Eye of mint. Out the kitchen window, no clouds. Clouds are rare.

"You'll have to water them, mostly," I say. "When I'm working, I'm not here much."

"When do you bring the Meters in?" she says.

"Tomorrow."

"Watch this." She takes another sip of water, pours the rest of the glass down the drain.

"What the hell," I say.

"You're panicking," she says. "I *knew* you were one of those types." She turns on the faucet and lets it run.

"What are you doing?" I lean over and put my hand on top of hers, twist the knob to off.

"Fucking with you," says Willa. "You haven't noticed? You haven't even noticed. I rigged it." She turns the kitchen faucet on again. Then she turns it on higher, to full blast. The red digits on the Meter move up by one.

"I rigged all the Meters," she says. "The shower, too. Every hundred units, it'll move up only one."

"A hundred to one?"

"Something like that," she says. "Maybe ninety. Eighty-five. Crazy, right?"

"When'd you do this?" I say, putting my hand in the stream of water.

"Last night. When you went in your room."

"Will they find out?"

"Nope. I've done it before. At my old place." She's happier than I've seen her. My giver of water. "My ex showed me how."

I tell her I am so happy. My Willa, my water. I tell her over and over. I'm drunk on mint. I tell her: I grew up in New Hampshire, with green all around. My father stayed in his study in the evenings, my mother downstairs at our piano, me in my room at my laptop and phone. We were a family of objects more than we were humans. My mother's sheet music, the sound of my father's door closing: Monday, Tuesday, Wednesday. Meals or a concert together. A plain life, yet so much to have. A collection of isolated acts. And our yard was greener than green, and when I sit in my yard of rock here, all I can do is will it green.

When Isaac comes over, I tell him what's happened. We can both shower after sex, not just use the sink. And he does, showers for three minutes, the water hitting his body, soft as hands. In the living room, Willa reads a magazine on the couch and drinks water. I introduce them. He sits with her. I bring us both glasses of water.

"Oh, we're doing this now?" he says. "Drinking whenever?"

"We're doing this," says Willa. "We're really doing it." She holds up her water. "To the good stuff!"

"To Meters and people who fuck with them!" Isaac holds up his glass.

Something in Willa gets excited by him in the room. I see it. I'm prettier, I decide in a juvenile moment. I'm what he likes, brunette, curvy, petite, and Willa's blonde and willowy. He's wearing that T-shirt of the band I don't know.

We tell Willa about Then What. We've never told anyone. Willa, what happens when the water's gone?

"Mexico," she says.

"Then what?" I say.

"And then we find a pool. We sit at the bottom and open our mouths."

"We could do that lots of places," says Isaac. He puts his full water glass down on the carpet. I wonder if he doesn't know how to bring himself to drink it.

"By the time I got here," I say. "They'd already drained the pool and hot tub."

"Well, yeah," says Willa. "How much money do you think they're going to let you swim in?"

She tells Isaac her dream about sex with the wolf and comes to the part where she stopped before.

"The rest will disgust you." She looks at me. "Susannah will judge me."

"How do you know that?" I say.

"I can tell. You're much more genteel than I am." To Isaac she says, "What's it like to be with someone that sweet?"

He looks at her. He's interested in her, in what she has to say.

"I can't get a read on her," Isaac tells me later in bed, taking off his glasses and balancing them on the nightstand.

"Because she's a stranger," I say. But she isn't. I think, she has never been a stranger to me.

At the Water Center the next day, everything works. We bring in the kitchen and bathroom Meters. Isaac's come, too. He wants to see if we get caught. I estimate we're double our water quota. A girl, twenty or so, in a collared shirt and nametag, scans bar codes on the Meters into a computer. She gives us fifty dollars cash for being less than our quota on the kitchen Meter.

"The city of Las Vegas thanks you," she says.

Willa smiles at her.

"My name's Ashley," the girl says. "I'm supposed to say that bullshit. But you know, good job."

"Well, that does it," Isaac says to Willa when we're back in her station wagon. "You're a genius." He rolls down the window. "A fucking genius!" he yells to the parking lot, sweat on his nose, sweat even on his lenses.

"Let's go to the man in the tent behind Atomic Liquors," I say with the cash in my hand. "Jesus, let's get a birdbath. We'll fill it up."

"You're cute." Willa looks behind her to drive out of the lot, but she's looking at me. She reaches and pats my knee. I take her hand and hold it. She lets me, she lets me more.

"Then what happens?" Isaac turns to me. He's smiling as I've never seen him, with genuine joy. Willa takes back her hand.

"All the pigeons come back," I say.

"All of California's pigeons," says Isaac.

"And all the birds in California and Utah!" I put my hands on his shoulders. "And hawks! And linnets! And nightingales. And eagles. And woodpeckers. And sparrows."

"Sparrows! I love sparrows!" Isaac shouts. "Then what?"

"Jays," I say. "Blue jays. And rain."

"Rain?" says Willa.

"Birds bring it with them," I say.

When I return from work at three a.m., Isaac's there, with my red Japanese flower robe on over his T-shirt and jeans, his glasses sinking on his nose, watering our line of green in the kitchen with Willa. Help us, they say. They're your children, too, says Willa. I've got to go to sleep, I say, kissing them both on the cheek. I have work tomorrow. Someone has to make money for our babies.

The next few days, Isaac isn't in bed when I wake up; he's with Willa, talking or watering the plants. He's unabashedly comfortable with her, something in him springing up. Springing open. He's a waiter on the Strip, and I hear him tell her he hates it. Just like that: he hates it. I don't ask what they do in the day. I don't know where her money comes from. I like thinking she just has it. She's always in the apartment when I wake up. When I'm home from work in the early morning, she and Isaac are asleep on the couch in front of the TV.

Willa and I water the ferns, the herbs. She's found a glass pitcher in one of the cabinets. I tell her about my ex-husband and his fiancée in Venice. He left me in New York two years ago, fled to Florence first, with Marisol. Now Venice. Mariner, I call him, with his Marisol.

"You don't need him," says Willa.

"I've got *you*," I say. "You're here."

"Yeah," she says. "And this." She turns on the faucet and lets it run. The Meter moves up one unit.

I imagine a miniature version of myself walking through the forest of the herb garden, leaves upright, a green-gold-green above.

"If they ever make an amusement park here," I say. "It should have tons of trees."

She refills the pitcher, waters the mint, blooming in mint-bright clusters. I think I see mint grow as water hits the leaves. My green. My green Willa. She did all of this.

"How much do you like him?" says Willa. "Isaac. Give me a number, one to ten."

"God, I don't know," I say. "Thirty thousand units."

"That's it?"

"That's all we have a month," I say. "That's love."

That week Willa asks to borrow fifty dollars, and I give it to her. She comes with me to the club, has made herself up with gold eyes like mine. My Willa in a green dress. She watches me sing from the bar. A couple of members of the band tell me they think she's fantastic looking, sexy, "the right amount of edge." When I'm halfway through a Gershwin number, I see Goodyman up at the bar, chatting with her. He's the kind who comes to the club in his three-piece suit from work. He buys her a water, gives her a roll of flush tokens she puts in her bra. He sends a kiss to me in the air.

During a break in sets, I go out on a backstreet of the Strip for a smoke in the desert dirt. There's a man singing outside, bellowing with deep dust in him. I hide my water bottle in my purse. He's always there. Peeling toenails, sandals the color of the road. Dressed in layers of holey rags coming apart at the shoulders, descending in flaps like a brown and rust tulip unpetaling. I put a toilet flush token in his hand. He puts his other hand around mine and holds on for a second. I give him another token. I don't know how he's here. By law, they shipped all of Vegas's homeless out to Utah months ago.

Someone's followed me. It's Goodyman, a full drink in his hand. He's got on a bright white shirt, black vest, the material straining over his pooch of a belly.

"Little girl," he says. "You giving away your wares?" He takes a drink of an amber something in his glass. "Your tokens, Susannah? Your jetons? Toilet time?"

"How much you had so far?"

"Not a drop all week till tonight," he says. "Been sobering up."

"You're so good," I say, taking a cigarette sticking up out of his chest pocket and placing it behind my ear. "So, so good."

He's blocking the back door. "Hey," he says. "Come here." He puts an arm around me, we start swaying. "Hey. I've got a sincere question for you." He fingers the star on my forehead. "You a lesbo?" he says. "A lesbarina?" He laughs and kisses my neck.

"Where's your jacket?" I push him away.

"My little lesbarina?" He catches my hand. Leans down and kisses the star.

"Who's asking?"

"My wife. She might want to fuckaroo you."

"Aw, Goody," I say, putting my arm around him. "No thanks."

"No? You say no?"

"It's a fine gesture."

"You little messed-up bitch," he says, pushing off my arm. "You too occupied with that girl? Wilfred?"

"Don't talk about her."

"I don't know what kind of what she is," he says. "She drinks water like a witch. And she eats ice. I watched her." He dumps the rest of his drink on the ground in one stream. "Nobody needs ice."

In the lounge, Goodyman gone, but Willa there, I sing a whole hour. Someone coming in shouts that it's raining outside. Las Vegas gets four inches a year, you'll hear it said. Willa is a rainmaker. She is rain.

I am a rainmaker. Rain comes from my toes to my dried vocal cords to my mouth, and when I sing I hold Distraction in my lips. I sing for you. I turn the lights from gold to green to blue.

"They gave me a raise," I say to Willa. "They need good singers who'll sing without water. They won't pay me anywhere like they will here. We're going to watch this place dry up." I turn the faucet on and fill the pitcher and leave the water running.

"We'll *get* to watch this place dry up," she says. "And then they'll airlift us out. Won't that be crazy? Then what?"

"And then Venice," I say.

"No. Maybe Washington," she says.

"And then Wyoming."

"And then the water comes back," she says. "Lake Mead fills up again."

Willa doesn't have next month's rent. It isn't due, but she knows she won't have it. I find I don't care. I tell her I owe her everything. We water our garden in the kitchen. I tell her to tell me the dream. In the dream with the wolf she has sex with, she says, the wolf is dead and she realizes it after. After she's come. That's what she didn't want to tell. I say, Everyone has strange dreams.

She leans against the counter. I hear the water we've let run from the faucet overfilling the pitcher, running down the drain. She takes the pitcher away, leaves the water on. Now she dips down. She places her lips perfectly in the stream of water and drinks. Her lips move every few seconds. I bend, too. I put my face to hers, and she doesn't move.

I kiss her. I hold my mouth on hers while the water runs. She inhales, exhales. I feel the texture of her breaths in her tongue. I've wanted her tongue. I feel for her arm, hold it at the elbow while kissing her. Then feel lower to her wrist—I hold its tattooed eye. I mine for her air, her blue breath, the air of her life into mine.

The front door opens. Willa and I stand quickly; I wipe my mouth. It's Isaac, with his white button-down shirt and creased black pants from the restaurant.

"Hey," he says, putting his keys on the counter.

He smells of red wine and potato grease. I turn off the faucet.

"Want to go water?" He looks at me.

"We did that already," I say. "We did that."

"But," says Willa. "They always want more."

There they are in a line on the kitchen counter, an emerald-gleam, healthier, glossier, green fire and plumage. We fill the pitcher again and again. Green overflows on the counter. The Faucet Meter barely moves.

"Okay." Willa looks at Isaac. "Do you have it?"

He nods.

"Go get it," she says.

From outside the door, he brings in something large, wrapped in a quilted blue blanket used for moving. He wobbles and sets it down. Just you wait, he says. He begins to unwrap. Take a look, he says. It's from us, she says.

Inside the blanket is a stone birdbath that comes to my waist. For you, she says. Well, for us.

"This is real?" I say.

"For the birds," says Willa. "When they come."

Isaac and I stand the birdbath up in the living room. I fill the pitcher with water and pour it all into the birdbath's stone basin. Willa puts her arm in the water. She bends, drinks from the bath. Sleek tongue in the water. From the kitchen, I bring our plants, set them around the birdbath. We sit on the couch, me in the middle. Watch our shrine to green.

"We can always keep it filled," says Willa.

"We'll have to start pruning the ferns," I say.

"Our tots," says Isaac. "Our little ones."

"Our chickadees!" I say.

I say, if the water comes back, I'll plant grass in the yard. Then roses and ferns. Orchids and asters. We'll have peahens and hawks, and pigeons and jays, and we'll plant more seeds from the man in the tent, and we'll live outside, and on days with no rain, we'll breathe in the dust, and watch the grass grow.

ACKNOWLEDGMENTS

This book remains unfinished until I say the names that brought me here. Each name travels with me. Each sits beside me in my solitude at my desk.

First, cities and towns. In Louisiana: Baton Rouge, Effie, Marksville, and Vick. In California: Los Angeles and Berkeley. Iowa City, Iowa. Hamilton, New York. Washington, D.C. Las Vegas, Nevada.

I have spent some of my happiest days at residencies. How can I properly thank you, MacDowell Colony, Vermont Studio Center, and Djerassi?

So many thanks to the Rona Jaffe Foundation and Black Mountain Institute for believing in me, especially during some of my most difficult times.

Thank you to my agent, Jin Auh. This book *is* because of you.

To my past and present mentors—Mark Richard, Janet Fitch, Judith Freeman, Donald Revell, Claudia Keelan, Emily Setina, Adelaide Russo, Cole Swensen, Lyn Hejinian, and Charles Altieri.

I am luckier than I can say for having the following people in my life, many of whom read these stories and helped me through them, even in ways they (perhaps) don't realize: Colleen O'Brien, Carol Ko, Lee Pinkas, Brandon Krieg, Michael Rutherglen, Vu Tran, Susannah Luthi, Rachel Hochhauser, Amy Silverberg, Allison Gibson, Cara Blue Adams, Emily Nemens, Shelly Oria, Andrew S. Nicholson, Aurora Brackett, Mary Belle, Pamela Benham Cooper, Austin Ely, Brett Finlayson, Maegan Poland, Kathleen Bogart, Leah Houk, Ramzi Fawaz, and Mira Dalju.

Corinna Barsan, thank you for knowing and loving this book so richly. And for your deep friendship. Thank you to everyone at Grove Atlantic for bringing me into your family.

These stories would not have happened without TZC.

Nor without my father, Tibi; my mother, Marjorie; and my brother, Owen.

This book is for Lula Clark, my great-great-grandmother. She is buried in Effie, Louisiana, in a small cemetery of much green and many great souls.